Samuel Irenæus Prime

Letters from Switzerland

Samuel Irenæus Prime

Letters from Switzerland

ISBN/EAN: 9783744766029

Printed in Europe, USA, Canada, Australia, Japan

Cover: Foto ©Andreas Hilbeck / pixelio.de

More available books at **www.hansebooks.com**

INTERLACHEN AND THE JUNGFRAU.

Letters from Switzerland.

BY

SAMUEL IRENÆUS PRIME,

AUTHOR OF "TRAVELS IN EUROPE AND THE EAST,"
&C., &C.

NEW YORK:

SHELDON & COMPANY, 115 Nassau Street.

BOSTON: GOULD & LINCOLN.

1860.

CONTENTS.

CHAPTER I

BASLE AND THE RHINE.

CHAPTER II.

CONSTANCE AND ZURICH.

(5)

CHAPTER III.

THE MOUNTAIN TOPS

CHAPTER IV.

LUCERNE AND THE LAND OF TELL.

CHAPTER V.

PASS OF ST. GOTHARD.

CHAPTER VI.

GLACIERS OF THE AAR.

CHAPTER VII.

MOUNTAINS, STREAMS AND FALLS.

CHAPTER VIII.

A GLACIER AND AVALANCHE.

CHAPTER IX.

INTERLACHEN AND BERNE.

CHAPTER X.

MONKS OF ST. BERNARD.

CHAPTER XI.

FIRST SIGHT OF MONT BLANC.

SWITZERLAND.

CHAPTER I.

BASLE AND THE RHINE.

The Three Kings—Cathedral—Council of Basle—Puritan rules—Dance of Death—Seats in the Diligence—Supplement—The Rhine—An Alderman in trouble—Dining in haste—English manners—Girls in holiday dress—Falls of the Rhine—Niagara—Up the river—Old nunneries—Gottlieben—Prisons of Huss and Jerome of Prague.

 WITZERLAND, to be seen aright, must be entered from Germany. Many travellers rush from Paris to Geneva, and beginning with Chamouni and Mont Blanc come down from the greater to the less, tapering off with the beautiful instead of rising to the sublime. One lovely summer day in the early part of the month of August, we left Baden Baden, where we had been resting after a tour in Belgium, Holland, Prussia, Saxony, Saxon Switz-

(9) 1*

erland, **Austria,** Bavaria, and Bohemia, **and came by**
the Duke of Baden's railroad to Basle.

The hotel de *Trois Rois,* or, *Three Kings,*
was reluctant to receive us, so great was the rush
of company. Large as some of our own first class
hotels, it was crowded to overflowing, but we found
lodgings for three **at the top of the house. It** stands
on the very borders of the river Rhine, which
rushes by with a powerful current, and the verandah
in front overhanging the stream is **a pleasant** lounge
after a weary day of travel. Lodgings for three **gen-**
tlemen, **or in German, "fur** drei herren," we had
so often asked **for,** that we came to be called the
" Drei Herren," or " dry herring," as it sounded in
our English **ears.**

The **river forms a broad and noble stream** along
the sloping bank on **which the city** stands ; the Jura
mountains rise on one side, and the hills of the
Black Forest on the other, while the intermediate
region is richly **covered** with vegetation, and **the villas**
of a wealthy class of people who have retired **from the**
city, or who own the soil. **Basle is a goodly town, and**
if the people **have** some rigid notions of morality in the
judgment of travellers **of** easy virtue, it is refreshing
to come into **a** city where the shops are closed of a
Sunday, and every one is required to be **at home by**
eleven o'clock at night. A city that bore so conspic-

uous a part in the Reformation, and still cherishes the ashes of so many great and good men, ought not to lose its veneration for the spirit and principles of the past. In the *Cathedral*, now in process of renovation, we stood over the dust of the learned ERASMUS, read his epitaph in Latin, walked among the beautiful cloisters which have been burial places for the wise and good for more than *six* hundred years! where the monuments stand of Grynæus, and Meyer, and Œcolampadius, men who were mighty in the Scriptures, in the days when such men were few. We walked through the portal of St. Gallus, under the statues of Christ and Peter, and the wise and foolish Virgins, and admired the pulpit of three pieces of stone, carved with great skill and effect; and then we were led to the chamber where the Council of Basle held its sessions, beginning in 1436, and lasting eight years. It has undergone no alterations in the four hundred years which have since elapsed. In the *Library* are preserved manuscripts of Luther, Melancthon, Erasmus and Zwingle, and a huge volume in which illustrious visitors had inscribed their names for two hundred years. The celebrated pictures of the *Dance of Death* once adorned the walls of the Dominican church in Basle, and a few of them still preserved are now hung up in this collection, among others of greater merit but less fame, by Holbein. A beautiful picture, which I have seen attempted with far less success before, presents a Venus sleeping by the side of a stream, and a skull lying near her, and flowers blooming around, to illustrate the lines: *Mortis imago sopor : velut amnis labitur ætas, vix forma reliquium pulvis et ossa manent.* "The image of death is sleep : like the river life glides away, and dust and bones, the only relics of departed beauty, are left behind." In the next room the same sentiment is more impressively taught from an uncovered sarcophagus, in which a female mummy grins horribly at you, as you look into the narrow house which she has slept in for two or three thousand years.

The architecture of this old Swiss town is very curious, and many of the most antique gateways and fortifications, towers and walls, remain to this hour, showing the quaint but not bad devices in the way of ornament, which were in use 450 years ago. In old times, too, they had moral laws here quite as stringent as those imputed to our New England ancestors. On the Sabbath, no one might go to church unless dressed in black ; the number of dishes and the quantity of wine for a dinner party were regulated by law, as well as the style and quality of clothes. The good people used to put religious mottoes over their doors, and one or two public houses still have them :

"In God I build my hopes of grace,
The ancient Pig's my dwelling place."

And another still more earnest :

"Wake and repent your sins with grief,
I'm called the Golden Shin of Beef."

The gates of the town are closed on the Sabbath day during the hours of service, and an outward respect paid to the day which is creditable to the people. In the hotel, a small room has been fitted up neatly as a chapel for an English service, a custom not unusual in Switzerland, where English travellers are flocking constantly.

Basle is the great starting point for Swiss travelling for those who enter the German frontier. We have now come to the end of railroads, and must depend on horses or go afoot. The sooner one takes his place in the *diligence* after arriving, the more likely he is to have a good seat when he wishes to depart, and though we were early for this, no less than twelve had the start of us, and the coach carried only nine. "You shall have a *supplement*," we were told, and at nine in the morning with twenty-five travellers we were at the *Post Office*, to be despatched with the mails and the females to Schaffhausen. This posting is a Government concern, and the postmaster has charge of the horses as well as the letters. There was no place but the middle of the street in which to remain, till at the appointed hour the heavy diligence lumbered up to the door: the nine predestinated thereunto took their seats ; an omnibus and one or two carriages by way of supplement, received the rest of us, many grumbling grievously that they had not places in the coach, and others preferring as we did, an easy carriage with a party of four. The postillion dressed in a yellow jacket with a brass horn under his arm, with which he amused himself and the country people as he passed, mounted the box, and we soon crossed the Rhine, and followed its banks upward for many a pleasant mile. The morning was fine after a rainy night, clear, cool and bracing ; the distant Alps were constantly in sight on the right, and the winding, often rapid, always beautiful river, with its vine-clad shores and smiling cottages was by our side. We left the carriage at *Lauffenburg*, and walked to the banks of the Rhine, where the river is choked into a narrow gorge, and dashes with terrible force through a deep sunk channel, among opposing rocks, making a fearful pass in which an English nobleman lost his life, attempting to make the rapids in a little boat. Resuming our seats, we found one of our fellow trav-

ellers belonging to the diligence, Alderman ———
of New York left behind. The coach was out of call,
and the best he could do was to mount the edge of
the postillion's single seat in front of our carriage and
ride on to the next post town. The Alderman was
heavy, the place was too strait for him, and I suggested that a *franc* would buy the whole seat. He
tried the effect of it, the postillion took the silver,
dropped down upon the foot rest, and the Alderman
had the seat to himself. In an hour we stopped to
dine. Perhaps we were here a few moments sooner
than mine host of the *Waldshut* Hotel expected us,
for the dinner was not on the table, but it gave us a
fine opportunity to observe a specimen of manners
sufficiently characteristic to be made a matter of
record. At the table there sat ten English, six German, and seven American ladies and gentlemen.
The dishes were slow in coming in ; the English gentlemen all having ladies under their care, left the
table, rushed into the kitchen, seized the best dishes
of meats they could find, brought them to their own
places, and helping themselves and their ladies, de-
voured them in the presence of the more barbarous
Germans and Americans, who looked on with amaze-
ment. I took the liberty of remarking that it was an
outrage, of which I had never before seen an example
in civilized life, and was happy to observe that the

practice was confined to a single nation out of the number represented here. An English lady gave me an approving nod, but the men were too far gone in beef and sour wine to pay any attention to lessons in good breeding. As might be expected, the leader in this grab-game grumbled at his bill, declared he was charged for more wine than he had drunk, and laid himself out in abusing Swiss taverns in general, and this in particular, till the postman's horn summoned him and the rest to their seats.

The scenery improves as we ascend the Rhine. The banks are steeper, the hills are bolder; the water rushes more rapidly through winding channels, and the people we meet bear more characteristic features of another country. It is a Catholic holiday. We are meeting the peasantry in great numbers, dressed in their best clothes, some of them gaily; blooming lasses in snow white muslin and no bonnets, but sweet pretty head-dresses and pink ribbons tied as pretty girls in all countries know how to tie them; they are gathering at the churches, and as they wend their way through green fields to the highway, they give a romantic air to the rural picture we are looking on. Many of them are paired, and as they saunter along hand in hand, and now and then with an arm thrown lovingly round the waist, we know them as probably paired for life, and send up a little prayer that they may jog along as pleasantly all the way through.

"The finest Cataract in Europe" is at Schaffhaus-sen. We arrived at sunset, just in time to see the falls before the last rays had faded into night. The Rhine is here 300 feet broad, and after foaming and rushing furiously for a mile or two it takes a bold leap over a shelving precipice sixty feet high, and plunges into a bay of waters below, boiling like a mighty caldron and sending up perpetual clouds of spray. In the midst of the cataract two columnar rocks rise perpendicularly, dividing the fall into three unequal parts. One of these rocks is clothed with shrubbery and the steep banks on either side are lined with trees. A castellated mansion crowns the summit on one side, and several buildings grace the other, so that nature and art have here combined to make a picture of wild romantic beauty, in which there is enough of grandeur to entitle it, at times, to be called sublime. Certainly we should so pronounce it, if we had not seen the waterfalls of America.

The only place to see a fall to perfection is directly in front of it. We are told to cross the river and go up the hill to a jutting crag and there in the midst of the spray, contemplate the "hell of waters," roaring and tumbling madly on their way into the dreadful deeps below. We went over, but nothing satisfies me but to see a waterfall from its base. It was an easy matter to induce two stout oarsmen to put the nose of their skiff into the teeth of the cataract, and drive her up as near to the falling torrent as their strength would fetch her. I knew the strong current would send the little shell down stream, like an arrow, when they crossed the eddies and struck the channel ; and so it proved. We toiled on till the spray-like rain covered us, and there we looked up at the white waves as they marched in fury down upon us, threatening to overwhelm the frail bark tossing on the surface as a shell. When we had studied the scene from various points of view, we returned to the shore and met a party of English gentlemen and ladies at Castle *Worth*, which commands a fine sight of the falls. "How does it compare with Niagara," one of them enquired of me. I replied, "We do not love to make comparisons between these beautiful scenes and those we have left at home. Nature there is more majestic in her works, and there is no sight on earth where so much majesty crowned with beauty is revealed as in the cataract of Niagara. You see that hill which bounds this valley on the west and that higher one which shuts it in above where the Rhine comes down : those hills are not so far asunder as the river of Niagara is at the moment it falls! It is a lake broader than this beautiful vale and the precipice to whose brow it comes is loftier than the turrets of that castle, now fading from our view. It comes not creeping down the rocks like *that*, but gathering itself up and with one mighty leap, clearing the barrier, it pours its awful flood, as if an ocean had been spilled, into the abyss below. In the moonlight and in the sunshine rainbows are twined upon its brow, and garlands of diamonds hang from the summit to the base, in beauty indescribable."

We climbed up to the hotel Weber, which stands on the brow of the hill, and the good man of the house gave us a chamber in full view of the falls, where we went to sleep with the roar of the tumult of many waters in our ears, making music the last we heard at night, and the first in the morning. Now the grandeur of the distant Alps began to appear. Long ranges, peak towering above peak, are seen; the names of some of them are familiar, as they stand there inviting us to come to their feet. Let us go.

Aug. 16.—Refreshed by a sweet sleep, and ready for another fine day, we were taken after breakfast to the village of Schaffhausen, where a small steamboat received us for *Constance*. The current of the Rhine above the falls is not so swift as below, but

the waters are the same deep green, increased
by the reflection of the beautiful sloping banks,
covered with luxuriant vineyards. The vines are
trained on short upright poles, not on arbors as with
us, and at a distance they look not unlike our corn
fields. But the river is so narrow here that we seem
to be in the midst of them, and enjoy the labors of
the dressers, as they work in the sun. Now we are
passing the old nunneries of Paradies, and Kather-
inethal, and that ancient castle above the town of
Stein is Hohenlingen, once the abode of the masters
of all this soil. Here is the island of *Reichenau*,
where the remains of an ancient monastery are seen,
and on the right as we are ascending is the castle of
Gottlieben, where John Huss and Jerome of Prague
were confined in gloomy dungeons from which they
were dragged to trial and death.

And this brings us to CONSTANCE.

CHAPTER II.

CONSTANCE AND ZURICH.

A decaying Town—the Kaufhaus—Famous Council—Dungeon of Huss—
Scene of Martyrdom—House of Huss—Lake Constance—the Ride to
Zurich—Villages—the Valley—Hotel Baur—a Swiss Cottage—the Fur-
nishing—Miles Coverdale—Zwingle—Lavater's Grave—the Library—Sunset View from the Botanical Garden.

 ORTY thousand people once lived together within the walls of Constance. Now less than seven thousand are here. But the old and curious houses still stand, many of them without inhabitants, and the whole city apparently asleep at noonday as we entered. The historic intere t hanging about Constance is very great, and will always render it attractive to the traveller. On the borders of the lake of Constance, and but a very few feet from the landing, we saw

(21)

the *Kaufhaus*, built in 1338, and memorable as the place in which the great "Council of Constance" sat in 1414–18, whose decision for good and for evil were so momentous in the Church of Rome. We walked up the solid steps into the second story, one wide low room supported by heavy wooden pillars, and with a rough plank floor like that of a barn. Here, in this room, more than four hundred years ago were assembled from all parts of the Christian world, no less than thirty cardinals, four patriarchs, twenty archbishops, one hundred and fifty bishops, two hundred professors of theology, besides princes, ambassadors, civil and ecclesiastical, abbots, priors, and inferior churchmen. The chair in which the Emperor Sigismund sat, and the chair in which the Pope presided, stand as they stood then, and various relics of those times, historically associated with the Council, are gathered, forming a Museum of unusual interest. Before this council John Huss and Jerome of Prague were brought from their dungeons, and though the Council was assembled professedly to reform the church, it condemned these holy men to the flames.

The old Cathedral is here, where those martyrs stood when the sentence of death was passed upon them, and the model of the dungeon not three feet wide and ten feet long, with the identical door and window in it, where Huss was confined for many weary months. Here too is the hurdle on which he was dragged to the place of execution, and when we had examined these and many interesting objects which a Catholic claiming to be the friend of Huss showed us, we walked out of the old chamber, and following the long street to the Huss Gate, found beyond the walls of the town, in the midst of a garden, the spot where these blessed men were caught up by chariots of fire into heaven. An old Capuchin convent, deserted now, is standing near it, and so peaceful and fertile seemed these fields as we stood in the midst of the fruits and flowers, it was hard to believe an infuriated mob had once rioted here, and religious persecution kindled the fires of martyrdom on the flesh of men of whom the world was not worthy.

In the Council Chamber are wax figures of these martyrs, bearing the records which I copied. "Jerome of Prague, called Faulfisch, a learned man of great celebrity, the friend and defender of John Huss, born at Prague, March 14, 1362; burned alive in consequence of the order of the Council of Constance, May 30, 1417, in the 55th year of his age. Jerome walked to the place of punishment, as though he went to a place of rejoicing. When the executioner was going to set fire to the pile behind him, Jerome said to him, 'Come here, light it before me, for if I had feared the fire, I would not have been here.'"

"John Huss, of Housenitts in Bohemia, born July 6, 1373, rector of the University and lecturer at Prague, burned alive at Constance in consequence of the order of the Council, July 6, 1415, in the 42d year of his age. His last words were, 'I resign my soul to the hands of my God and my Redeemer.'"

Returning from the place of execution, we paused in front of the house in which John Huss lodged before he was imprisoned. A rude image in stone of the Reformer, but a strongly marked likeness, was on the outside. Every one we met could tell us which way to go to find the Huss house, and though there are but a few hundred Protestants in the whole city, the idea seemed to be general that a good man was wrongfully and cruelly murdered when Huss was burned.

In the after part of the day, as the shades of evening were drawing around us, we had a boat and went out on the Lake, and skirted along its shores, passing a large monastery where a few brothers of the Augustine order are still maintained, and a few miles beyond is a long and beautifully planted nunnery which was suppressed in 1838, and converted into a hospital, though the sisters are permitted to live and die there, without adding to their number. This is the largest of all the Swiss lakes, and lies 1255 feet above the level of the sea. We floated around until the evening became so cool that we were glad to go ashore. Passing an ancient-looking church of which the door was standing open, we walked in : a solitary lamp was burning near the altar, and the sound of voices led us down the aisle to a door opening into one of the cloisters where a group of boys were on their knees, repeating prayers in concert, and vieing with each other in the loudness and sing-song tone with which they performed the service. We returned to our hotel by the light of lamps hung in the middle of a chain stretched across the street, and went early to bed as we were early to rise.

Aug. 17.—We went by diligence to Zurich to-day. The ride was pleasant. Some of the Swiss towns we passed through were very pretty, showing so much taste in the grounds about the houses, that one was sure there was a pleasant home. Part of the way was called the Roman road, and the remains of the ancient presence of that people are still visible. The river *Thur* flows along in the valley of the road, and its banks are lined with frequent mansions. Chateaus of elegance are on the hill-sides, and just after leaving Constance we passed one in which the present Emperor of France once resided, and which still belongs to him. *Frauenfeld* is a fine town where we paused to dine, and I there celebrated the day as an anniversary that **I am quite** sure was not forgotten elsewhere. *Winterthur* is really a beautiful city. Its streets intersect one another at right angles, and each intersection has an arched gateway, surmounted by a tower with a clock. **As we advance** into Switzerland, **the scenery becomes more** commanding: now and then a sharp blue **peak shoots up into the sky, and** as the road descends **we** lose sight **of it** again, to see the same and others as **we rise. At last** as the day was closing, we came suddenly **upon** ZURICH, the capital of the canton of the same name, the **most** thriving city in Switzerland, and rejoicing in the midst of one of the most beautiful valleys in the world. I should be deemed extravagant were I to speak of it as it appeared to me when descending **through** vineyards and gardens, **and** among elegant mansions, to the shores of the lake on which this city **stands.** The Hotel *Baur* is the largest and best in the town, but it was crowded, and the gentlemanly landlord said the best he could do for us was to give us rooms in **a** private house adjoining his own. To this we assented with the more readiness, as it would bring us at once into the residence of the Swiss, and we could see more of their indoor life than the hotel would furnish. There is no carpet on the floor, except a beautiful square on which the centre-table with a pot of flowers is standing. A piano with music and books is on one side, a sofa covered with white dimity on the other. The chamber looks out on a square, and the windows fill the entire front of the room, but rich lace curtains hang before them, and some of the panes of glass are replaced with porcelain pictures of exceeding loveliness. Before the mirror is suspended a vase, like a pendant lamp, in which a plant is growing, with its leaves as on silver threads falling gracefully on every side of it. Another flower-pot has a plant trained upon a flat frame, in the centre of which is one of these porcelain pictures through which the light is streaming. Around the walls are many engravings in neat frames, and on the mantel and side-tables are various ornaments, chiefly curiously carved figures in wood, or beautiful glass-work, all displaying the taste of their possessor, and telling us all the time that these are the domestic precincts of some one who has let the lodgings for a season. These delicate cushions of pink silk with white lace edging, assure me that a lady is the rightful tenant; but I am tired, and shall slip into the linen sheets. Good night.

Aug. 18.—To-day we have been exploring Zurich, a city famous in the history of the Reformation and dear to every Protestant heart. Here the exiles of England, when Bloody Mary was on the throne, found a hiding-place from her bitter persecutions. Here the first entire English version of the Bible, by *Miles Coverdale*, was printed in 1535. From my window I see the cathedral where Zwingle, the soldier of the Reformation who resisted unto blood **striving against sin, once thundered the wrath** of **heaven upon the** abominations **of the Church of** Rome. Here is the house yet standing in which he passed the last six years of his noble life. The clock of St. Peter is now striking. This church had for its pastor for twenty-three years the celebrated *Lavater*, author of the work on Physiognomy. He was born here, and in the door of the parsonage which I visited to-day, he was shot by a brutal soldier, when the town was taken by the French in 1799. He had **given wine and** money to his murderer but a few minutes before : and though he lingered for three months, he refused to give up the name of the assassin to the French commander, who desired to punish the atrocious deed. I plucked a flower and a sprig of myrtle from his grave in the humble churchyard of **St. Anne, where** a simple tablet to his memory bears this inscription : " **J. C. Lavater's Grave.** Born 15th Nov. 1741. Died 2d Jan. 1801." In the town library of 45,000 volumes, admirably arranged, is a

fine marble bust of Lavater, and also of Pestalozzi,
with portraits of Zwingle and many other reformers.
But I was more interested in reading several manu-
script letters in Latin, by Lady Jane Grey, Joanna
Graia, addressed to Bullinger. The beautiful execu-
tion of the writing, the quotations in Greek and
Hebrew, the spirit they breathed, and the fate of
their lovely author, gave them sacred interest.
Here, too, in his own Bible is the family record of
Zwingle and his wife Anna Bullinger; and many
Greek and Arabic manuscripts which Dr. Raffles or
Dr. Sprague would give a heap of guineas to get.

It is said that the sunset view of the city, valley,
lake, and mountains is not surpassed by any scene in
Switzerland. We had been so busy in these old and
interesting scenes, that the day was gone before we
knew it, and as we walked out to climb the hill, from
which the view is to be had, we feared the sun had
already set. Part of the old rampart of the town
remains, an elevated mound which has been tastefully laid out with walks and planted with shrubs
and flowers, for a botanical garden. On the summit
fine shade-trees stand, and here is one of the most
beautiful promenades in the world. The sun was
half an hour high, and just as we reached the hill-
top it began to come down from behind a dense
cloud, like a mass of molten gold distilled into a

transparent globe. Its liquid form appeared to tremble as it came forth; but the face of nature smiled in his returning beams. The nearer summits first caught the brightness, and then the more distant, invisible before, now stood forth in their majesty, shining in the sunlight. Below me lay the lake like a silver sea. And all along its shores and far up the hill-sides, thousands of white cottages and villas, the abodes of wealth and peace and love, sweet Swiss homes, rejoiced in the sunshine, as they sent up their evening psalm of praise from ten thousand happy hearts to God. A hundred years hence our valleys may be so peopled : but we have none now like this. For a thousand years these hill-sides have been tilled, and all these acres, wrested from the forest, and subdued by the hand of industry and art, have been planted with corn and wine, neat and many splendid mansions have been reared in every nook and on every sunny slope, and now on all sides the panorama seems to present the very spot where learning, religion, taste and peace would delight to find a refuge and a home. It is now sunset in the valley. The lake is dark. The last ray has played on the spire of St. Peter and the Minster. But the dome of the Dodi still gleams in the sun, and the far-off Glarus and Uri are reflecting his lingering beams.

They are gone. The rose-tints have faded from the loftiest summit of snow, and the sun has gone down to rise on those dearer to me than his light, in a distant land.

CHAPTER III.

THE MOUNTAIN TOPS.

AUGUST 19.

ANKIN challenged me this morning to walk to the heights of Utleberg, on the Albis ridge, to the west of Zurich. The Utleberg is only three thousand feet high! and that is a small matter in Switzerland. After a cup of coffee we set off at eight in the morning, and without guide or mules we wandered out of the town, across the river, and through beautiful vineyards, with luxuriant grapes, not ripe enough to be tempting. We climbed along up the hill-side.

(32)

Other parties were on their way, some German, some French, some English, none American but ourselves. At the foot of the hill we met a flock of milk white goats, which their owner was driving down from the mountains to sell in town; beautiful creatures; for the first, we learned that beauty could be affirmed of a goat. Here the lame and the lazy supplied themselves with mules, and a comical figure of a fat German lady on a miserable little donkey, will be an amusing memory for many a day. When she was half way up the mountain she looked so jaded with the jerking, that we thought she would have suffered less if she had carried the donkey. We cut stout sticks in the forest, and pushed on, stopping now and then to pick flowers, or to examine a leech or a lizard, in the pools and streams by the side of the path, resting when tired, but pressing onward and upward, steadily and slowly; encouraged often by the splendor of the scene below, as we caught it from some opening in the woods, and feeling that we had the day before us and nothing else to do. The ascent became steeper as we pressed along, and it doubtless seemed steeper to us the more we were wearied with the way, but we made it in less than two hours, winding around the mighty rock that caps the apex, and entered the house of refreshment before we looked off into the world below.

2*

I had not felt myself in Switzerland till on this summit, we saw for the first time a real Alpine view. It has *points* of view peculiar to itself, nationally characteristic; there is nothing got up on the same scale and the same plan in any other part of God's great world. Why it pleased him to heap these hills in such " confusion unconfused," in this little country, we do not know, but they who would see the most remarkable of his works in mountain-building, must come here and climb up to some of the highest peaks, where they can take in at once as much of the majesty of the scene as each man's mind can hold. Rankin and I reasoned some time on the question whether these lofty ranges were clouds in the heavens or mountains propping up the sky. Now the problem is solved. What we thought might be white clouds, are the snowy ridges of the distant hills, and the dark blue mountains are now facing us as from one height across the valley we see them without looking up.

The vale of Zurich lies at our feet. The lake for twenty-five miles, and with a breadth of not more than three, stretches itself more like a river than a lake, through the valley to the south as far as we can see ; and the hills rise very gradually from the water affording the most delightful grounds for vineyards ; while scores of villages, each with its church spire, are scattered on each side, and between the villages so many dwellings are seen, that the whole valley, with its dense population, seems but one great family; certainly, it is one neighborhood, where industry, religion, intelligence and happiness, ought to flourish and have their reward. Thalwyl may be seen away to the south, near to which Lavater wrote a portion of his work on Physiognomy; and still farther on is Richtensweil, where Zimmerman lived, whose work on "Solitude" celebrates the praises of this spot. So does Klopstock in his ode, and Gessner, the Swiss poet, who was born in Zurich and has a monument reared to his memory in one of its delightful promenades. There, too, is Stafa, where Goethe once resided, and Rapperschuyl, with the longest bridge in the world, it is said, four thousand eight hundred feet, or three-fourths of a mile; but I think the Cayuga bridge is longer. There lies a beautiful islet, in which Ulrich Von Hutten, the friend of Luther, found a refuge and a grave. Look away to Usnach, and you see a valley out of which the river *Linth* is flowing; connected with it is a remarkable story. Yesterday in the churchyard of St. Anne, we saw a massive rough stone, with a polished spot in the midst of it, on which was engraved in gilt letters, "Escher, Von der Linth," or Escher of the Linth. The title had plainly been given him for some work connected with the Swiss river of that

name. Some thirty or forty years ago the river,
coming down from the glaciers, and bringing with it
a vast quantity of stones and soil, had become so
much obstructed, that the valley was repeatedly over-
flowed, terrible pestilences followed, and the inhabitants swept off in great numbers. Conrad Escher
suggested to the government the idea of digging a
new bed for the river, and turning its waters off into
another lake, the Wallenstadt, where its deposits
would be received without injury. This lake he connected with that of Zurich by a navigable canal, and
so complete was the success of all his suggestions,
that he is looked upon as a national benefactor. Just
there, at the opening of the valley, a tablet has been
placed in the solid rock, with an appropriate inscription. But that is not all. Hard by it is an institution
for the education of the poor of the canton, which is
called after his name ; and a factory where the Linth
colony are at work, who were brought here and supported while the great work was in progress on which
they were employed.

Whichever way the eye turns from this point of
observation, it finds something interesting or wonderful on which to rest. We are now in the morning of
our tour in Switzerland, and have been assured again
and again that this is *mere* beauty, compared with
the glory that awaits us hereafter. But those mighty

mountains crowned with eternal snow, and piercing the very skies with their sharp peaks, or supporting the heavens with their broad white shoulders, are certainly most majestic works of God, and what more and greater there can be, it is beyond imagination to conceive. Not many travellers climb up here. They are in such haste to see the Rigi and the Passes, and the Vale of Chamouni, that they do not give a day to Zurich, the most classic and picturesque of any of the cantons of Switzerland. An English gentleman and lady are up here with me, who have just been traversing this whole country on foot. They are full of delight with the view, though they have seen everything else that is to be seen.

The only incident to give variety to our return was losing the way, and making the walk a mile longer; but that was of small account to Swiss pedestrians, ambitious of doing great things, and making nothing of climbing a mountain, and coming down before dinner.

We are at Zurich now. Mr. *Baur* has the most elegant " Hotel and Pension " on the verge of the Lake of Zurich, that I have seen in Europe. He calls this, as well as the Hotel in front of the Post Office, after his own name, and gives them a degree of personal attention unequalled by any landlord into whose hands it was ever my pleasure to fall. In most of the hotels in Europe, the proprietor keeps himself out of sight, and trusts the entire management of affairs to his assistants, the head waiter being the most of a man you are ever able to find. Mr. Baur is everywhere at once: receives his guests on their arrival, makes himself acquainted with their wants, and sees that they are attended to without fail. His new house on the lake with a charming garden in front, is one of the most delightful places for a weary traveller to rest in for a few days.

There are many routes to the Rigi. Of course we went by the best. Every traveller does; at least he thinks so, and that often amounts to the same thing. But in this as in every other road up hill in life, before a man gets half way up, he wishes he had taken the other. So it matters little, if he only reaches the top at last. The steamboat on the Zurigsee, leaves at eight in the morning, and at least a hundred passengers crowded the little thing, when with a lovely breeze and a fine clear day we were off for the Rigi.

The glory of the Rigi is at sunset and sunrise, and then there is none unless the sky is clear. Nor are you sure of a clear sky up there, if it were ever so bright when you left the base. The group of mountains known by the name of Rigi, of which the highest peak is alone the object of interest to the traveller, stand so isolated by the lakes of Zug and

Lucerne from the rest of the ridges and ranges, that the view from the summit, especially at the close of the day and at sunrise, is unequalled. It stands up there alone, as an observatory from which to see the others. An hour on the boat brought us to the village of Horgen, where we were carried by stages across the country to Zug, on a lake of the same name. At Horgen about sixty passengers were landed, and we found that our tickets had been numbered as they were given to us on board the boat, and we were to be seated in the coaches accordingly. My number was forty-seven, very near the end of the list, but it turned up a very good seat, on the shady side of the stage, a very important matter in the middle of a hot day for a ride of three hours. Not a winding but very much of a zig-zag road, led us over the hill country that divides the lakes. Sometimes we had delightful views, deep ravines through which the mountain streams were finding their way; on the crest, the Rigi and Pilatus first meet the eye, and then rapidly we make our way to the borders of the lake, on which stands the little town of Zug, the capital of the Canton of that name, the least among the tribes. After a hasty dinner at the tavern we embarked on another steamboat, and still smaller than the one on the Zurich Lake. What a lovely sheet of water is this Lake Zug! It lies eighteen hundred feet higher than the sea ; and all around it except at the head, the richly cultivated shores are sloping away from the water's edge. But just before us, as we are going South, the noble Rigi rises from the shore of the Lake, and in the clear water the whole of that vast mountain clothed with verdure to the very summit is reflected so perfectly, that instead of looking up to study the ridges and precipices and forests and flocks on its rugged sides, it is pleasanter to study it as it lies there in the depths of this pellucid sea. We reached the South end, or head of the lake about three in the afternoon, and here we arranged to ascend the mountain.

The ascent from Arth is made by many, but it is far better to push on through the village to Goldau, and there look at the evidences of the awful work of ruin and death that was wrought in 1806 by the slide of a large part of the Rossberg mountain; burying 450 human beings in one living grave. There is the fresh white side of the mountain, as if the half of it had fallen away yesterday. It is 5000 feet high ; and lies in great strata of pudding stone, which is very liable to be split asunder by the water that filters between the layers. You can see the ranges in the strata as the sun falls on this bare side, and it seems as if what was left lying there, might one of these days come down to find the half

that left it fifty years ago. Then a portion three
miles long and a thousand feet broad and at least a
hundred feet thick broke away from the rest, after a
long succession of heavy rains; and came down into
the valley, teeming with a population of happy
peasantry, and overwhelmed them with the most
awful deluge of modern times. So sudden was the
rush of rocks and earth, that a party of travellers
going up the Rigi, where I ascended, were met by
the torrent; seven had passed on 200 yards ahead of
the other four and were caught by the descending
avalanche, and never seen again. The valley is now
covered with vast rocks and masses of the con-
glomerate, which then came down, and with so much
force that some of them now lie scattered some
distance up the hill on the other side of the vale!
Fifty years have not restored the valley to its former
fertility and beauty. One of its lakes was nearly
filled up, and now little pools are seen where once
was the bed of a handsome sheet of water. The
stories told of individual cases of suffering, of whole
families perishing, and what is on some accounts
more distressing, of some being taken and others
left, are so many that I will not attempt to repeat
them now. I walked into the beautiful little church
at Goldau, a gem, and on each side of the front door
is a black slab with a record of names of some of

those who perished in that dreadful day. This is a Roman Catholic Canton, as I had evidence presently.

A new scene opens on the eye of the traveller when for the first time he arrives at the foot of a mountain with a large party, and prepares to ascend. We led off on foot from Arth to Goldau, supposing that the fifty or more from the boat would strike up the hill immediately. But they followed us: some with guides, some without: some carrying their own packs, others with a servant to help them: some were ladies ready to foot it to the summit: some were to be carried in a chair on a bier by four bearers: the lame and the lazy are expected to ride on horses. I was in the former class to-day, recovered from my Utleberg tramp, and was glad to have good company to keep me in countenance, for I was a little ashamed of myself in taking a horse when so many, and some of them ladies, were going up on foot.

. The path for a mile is gently ascending, and then takes a shaded gorge in the hills, and on this account is greatly to be preferred to those paths which lead from Arth and Weggis, around the mountain, exposing the pilgrim all the way, to the rays of the sun. Now we are mounting steadily: turning frequently in the saddle to look at the constantly enlarging and ennobling view. Now and then a little cascade diversifies the hour : or we stop to refresh ourselves from the many rills that are gurgling by the path. The noise of running streams and waterfalls is constantly heard, and on the stillness of the air the tintinabula or tinkling of the bells on the necks of the dun-colored cows, that are feeding in numerous herds all up the sides of the mountain, comes gently to the ear as soft music.

All along up the mountain are small sheds, called chapels or stations, with some rude image of the Saviour in it, and pilgrims, to whom indulgences were promised by the Pope in the seventeenth century, are going from one to the other stopping at each and saying their prayers. I dismounted and entered one ; where the most hideous sight met my eye which I have yet seen in the miserable Romish worship. A full life size figure of Christ sinking to the earth beneath the weight of the cross is carved in wood ; the countenance indicating agony, but such a horrid face to personate the Saviour ! and a wig on his head of long dirty hair hanging over his shoulders ! It was sickening, and I was glad to hasten away from it, as rapidly as possible.

These praying stations, thirteen in number, lead on to a neat church called " Mary of the Snow," and around it are lodging-houses for pilgrims who are very numerous in the month of August. A small

convent is here, where **four or five monks of the Ca-**
puchin order reside; they **do service** in the church,
and among the mountains **where their** priestly **aid is**
required. These lodging-houses are sometimes resorted to by invalids for the benefit of the mountain
air, and the whey of goat's milk, which can be had
in great abundance here. Beggars beset your path
from the valley to the mountain top: old **men** and
old women, young men and young women, and little
children trained to toddle into the road and put out
their hand before they can speak so as to be under-
stood. Many of these are not in want; but every
bit of money that can be extracted from travellers **is**
clear gain.

The steepest of the ascent is over, long before you
reach the summit, and the last mile of winding way
is a very easy and pleasant ride. The change of atmosphere **is great;** and an overcoat is needed at
once, if you are warm with walking. Fortunately
you have had no chance to get the view **for some**
time, till it bursts upon you all **at once as** you plant
your feet on the mountain **top, on a piece of** table-
land, of half an acre, that forms a magnificent platform from which to behold this scene. More than
two hundred people are there before us: most of
them parties travelling for pleasure from all parts of
the civilized world, with guides, couriers and serv-

ants, a singular group to find yourself among so suddenly and so far above the level of "the world and the rest of mankind." One large hotel, and one small one are to shelter this company for the night, and we are so fortunate as to find that we are to have a small room with three beds, just under the roof, with holes about the size of a hat to admit light and air! That is better than none, and some of these people will have none. Still the two hotels on the summit, and one half an hour down, the Rigi Staffel, afford abundant accommodations to company, unless as in the present instance, the weather has been bad for a week, and hundreds have been waiting for a fair day, and the promise of a good night above. The Album of the house in which visitors register their names records the disappointment of many who have climbed up to see nothing but that mysterious mist which so often shrouds the mountain tops. Probably the greater part of visitors are thus mocked, for it is cloudy up here more than half the time. One party thus groans:

> " Seven weary up-hill leagues we sped,
>   The setting sun to see ;
>   Sullen and grim he went to bed,
>   Sullen and grim went we.
>   Nine sleepless hours of night we passed
>   The rising sun to see,
>   Sullen and grim he rose again,
>   Sullen and grim rose we "

Not such was our fate. The sun was half an hour high when we reached the highest peak ; and the first Alpine panorama was around us. Other views had been partial : this was a great circle of the heavens and the earth, three hundred miles in circumference ! A few clouds in the western sky were gorgeously crimson in the declining sun, but the atmosphere was clear enough to reveal every mountain, every lake, every village, city, forest and plain, with the cottages innumerable, dotting the valleys. At our feet the Lakes of Lucerne and Zug are apparently underneath the mountain, and they stretch themselves so curiously among the hills, that we can scarcely determine to what sheets of water they belong, or whether they are new lakes and not those seen before. And away at a distance are other waters, some of them very small, but giving beauty and variety to the plains below. The villages lying close by have their historic interest. All this region is William Tell's. His name is associated with many a spot on which the eye is resting. A neat little chapel is built to mark the place where he shot his oppressor Gessler. Here at the right is the Lake and town of Zug, and just behind it, rises the spire of the church of Cappel, where Zwingle fell on the field of battle. But turning from the views at the West and North, and looking to the South and East, and such a prospect of Alps on Alps is seen as no one had believed could be piled into sight from a single point. The Bernese Alps clothed in perpetual robes of snow; those of Unterwalden and Uri, with the dull blue glaciers in the midst of them; sending up the peaks of Jungfrau, the Titlis, Rothstock and Bristenstock, are directly in front, and on to the Eastward, is the broad white head of the Dodi, the Sentis and the Glarish; but these are a few only of the many named and unnamed that are now reflecting the sunset from their white crowns, or retiring into the shades of evening as the sun goes down. We look to the South East into an opening called the Muotta Thal, where Suwarrow and Massena with their hostile armies fought bloody battles in the midst of fearful crags and precipices, and we wonder that this land of mountains and ice has been selected as the scene for so much warfare and blood. The sun was now sinking to the edge of the horizon. A lady standing near me said, "It is fit to light such a scene as this!" There was a fitness between the sun and the scene that was truly striking and glorious. The hum of the hundred voices was hushed. It was also fit that we should be still while the sun took his last look of our world that night.

It is for a wonder to me that Switzerland has pro-

duced so few poets, but not strange that some of the
noblest strains of English poetry have been penned
under the inspiration of these Alpine views. They
awaken a train of emotions so profoundly new,
and at the same time so elevating and sublime, that
the heart wishes to utter itself in the passionate language of poetry rather than in the duller words of
prose. "These are thy works," O God : before the
mountains were built, and before the hills, thou
wert here. Thou didst "prepare the heavens, the
earth, the fields, and the highest part of the dust of
the world." Thou hast weighed the Alps in a
balance, and held these mountains in the hollow of
thy hand. They shall flow down at thy presence,
when thou comest to shake terribly the earth. They
stand now, because thou, Lord, dost hold them up,
for giants as they are, and touching thy heavens, they
still lean on thee.

During this half hour of observation on the summit of the Rigi, we had been wrapped in our cloaks
to protect us from the cold. As soon as the sun was
gone, we were glad to go into the house, where a
table for a hundred guests was spread, with a hot
supper sufficient for half the number ; and before ten
o'clock we were sound asleep. Those who could not
find beds spent the night in the dining hall, entertaining themselves and disturbing the rest, but we were

so far above them that we heard nothing till the blast of a wooden horn rung through the halls, informing us that the sun would be up before us if we did not hasten to meet him. We hurried on our clothes, wrapped up warmly, and in a few moments stood with our faces to the East, intently watching, like worshippers of the Sun, the first signs of his coming. One single peak was precisely between us and the sun, and as the earliest tints of the morning began to redden it, the appearance was not unlike that of a kindling fire in the summit. The blaze gathered around it, and seemed to shoot away into the regions of ice and snow; and then far into the clouds above, the bright hues of day were cast, and the crowd stood still, anxious to enjoy the first view of the emerging sun. The horn was blown again by the trumpeter, a miserable mode of announcing that the King was coming, as if he needed a herald as he rode up the East in his chariot of gold and fire. There was just haze enough in the atmosphere to dim the sun of his dazzling brightness, and we could look steadily on his face as he rose behind the mountain, and seemed to pause on the summit, and calmly to look down on the world he had left in darkness a few hours before. Then peak after peak, and mountain ridges, and domes and minarets, fields of fresh snow, and forests of living green, began to

3

catch the morning tints: gorges in the hill sides would lie there in deep shadow, and bosoms of virgin snow, bared to the rising sun, would blush when he looked in upon them, while villages and hamlets in the vale below are still wrapped in the shades of the gray dawn, and have not thought of waking yet to begin another day. We spent an hour or two in the enjoyment of this magnificent prospect, which we are told is one of the most delightful we are to have in Switzerland; and when the sun was fairly up to the dwellers in the vale as well as to us on the mountain top, we turned our backs upon him, took a cup of coffee in the Rigi Culm, and bade farewell to the most splendid of all the prospects we had ever seen, or expect to see on earth. I am greatly moved in the presence of Niagara; and there have formed impressions of the active power and glory of the great Creator, such as are conveyed by no other of the works of God. But now I am looking on the silent evidence of his creating might in a new and wonderful form; and it seems to me but a short step from those shining glaciers and snow-crowned palaces to the central throne of Him who sitteth in the circle of the heavens. "O Lord God of Hosts, who is a strong Lord like unto thee? The heavens are thine: the earth also is thine; as for the world and the fulness thereof, thou hast founded them: the

north and the south thou hast created them; Tabor
and Hermon shall rejoice in thy name. Thou hast a
mighty arm; strong is thy hand, and high is thy
right hand."

As we had ascended the Rigi from Goldau, on the
eastern side, we now went down on the western to
Weggis. We were in no haste: the day was before
us, and we had nothing to do but to walk till we
were tired, choose a shady spot commanding a fine
view of the lake of Lucerne and the surrounding
hills, and then rest and enjoy the scene. The bells
from the herds of cattle far below us, and sometimes
above us, and the strains of music from the villages
in the vales, would come floating to us on the
morning air, while nature with all her voices was
making one rich psalm. The descent is far less
fatiguing than climbing up, but when continued for
two or three hours it becomes exceedingly exhausting. We provided ourselves with pike staffs having
a Chamois horn for a head, and with these we
resisted the too constant downward tendency, using
them as a drag to a wheel, and making the greatest
effort to hold back. On this path to or from the Rigi
is a boarding and bathing house, over a spring of
very clear cold water to which invalids resort; and
as walking on the mountain side for an hour or
so after bathing is part of the discipline, I have no

doubt that the establishment works many wonderful
cures. A chapel of the Holy Virgin is close by,
where prayers are daily said for the shepherds on the
precipices, whose lives are in constant danger while
they pursue the duties to which they are trained.
Half an hour below the chapel, the path leads
through a mighty archway formed by two huge
masses of rock supporting a third between them.
Some great convulsion of nature has thrown them
into this remarkable position, and they show in their
make the nature of all the upper strata of these hill
sides, which are in constant danger of sliding down
when the water works its way under them, and
separates them from the lower. Here we sat down
and refreshed ourselves: a cool breeze rushing
through the passage, and making a delightful resting
place for weary travellers.

I said it was easier far to go down than up. So it
is, but one who caries much weight, or who has not
considerable powers of endurance should be cautious
of making the experiment. A very heavy gentleman
who came to the foot of the mountain with us yesterday, and rode up, with his son, a fine lad of fourteen,
running along by the side of the horse, attempted to
come down on foot. We overtook him; and just
then he lay down on the grass by the side of a
beautiful spring of water : he was exhausted, and had

sent his son down for help. Presently the faithful and noble boy came running up the mountain with a bottle of wine and a loaf of bread, and soon four stout men with a chair, whom the lad had out-stripped, came on, and the heavy gentleman was carried by hand the rest of the way. I met them afterwards at the foot of the hill, and congratulated the father on his safe arrival; and more on being the father of such a boy.

CHAPTER IV.

LUCERNE AND THE LAND OF TELL.

The Lake—Avalanches—Pontius Pilate—Lucerne—Dance of Death—Fishing—
Storm on the Lake—Ramble among the Peasantry—Two Dwarfs—On the
Lake—Rifle Shooting—Chapel of William Tell—Scenes in his Life—Altorf
—Hay-Making—a Great Day.

N THE Hotel de la *Concorde*, the "house of peace," I found a pleasant chamber on the edge of the Lake of Lucerne; and so near that in its lucid waters I can from my window see the large fish chasing and devouring the little ones, just as big fish on land are doing everywhere. In front, the lofty Pilatus rises in heavy grandeur, and the Buochsherhorn and Stauzerhorn are in full view, with other peaks all white with snow, while it is oppressively hot below. I spent the day here at the foot of the mountain.

(54)

There is no life in this little settlement except when
the boat arrives with travellers for the Rigi: the
mountain comes down so suddenly to the shore
that there is hardly room for dwellings, and a
few inhabitants only are scattered along on the
water's edge. But it is on the shore of the most
enchanting lake in Europe, and at a point where
some of the finest views of this lake are to be had.
We sat on the bank to see the sun set, a sight of
which one never tires; hundreds of travellers have
passed up or down the Rigi to-day, and of that whole
number we are the only two who have cared to rest
here to study and admire the scenery, and at the
same time refresh ourselves for future pilgrimages.

There was a crash among the mountains just now:
at first we thought it the noise of a steamboat on the
lake, but the roar became quickly greater, and we
knew that it was an avalanche of ice or of rocks that
had come down the side of old Pilatus. It was the
first that we had heard, and were very willing that
the quiet of our evening should be thus disturbed.
Then as if nothing were to be wanting to make the
enjoyment of this scene perfect, the clouds mar-
shaled themselves about the Buochsherhorn and
played off their lightnings around his head; while
torrents of rain came down on the lake below us,
and the snow fell in sheets on the loftier mountains

in the South. This lake is subject to sudden visitations of storms, and is therefore dangerous for skiffs unless under the guidance of the native boatmen, who know the signs of the weather, and put in for shore when they apprehend the approach of a gale. The hoary mountain *Pilatus* is said to have derived its name from Pontius Pilate, who was driven away from Rome, became a wretched wanderer here in this wild land, and finally in the horrors of a guilty conscience plunged from one of the crags of this mountain into the lake and perished. From its peculiar position and great height, 7,000 feet above the sea, and the foremost in the Alpine chain at the North, the clouds delight to gather about it, and so many are the storms which come down from this point, the superstitious dwellers on the shores for a long time supposed that poor Pilate was at the bottom of them all, and the lake would never be safe till his troubled spirit was put to rest.

From the summit of the Rigi, the seven towers of Lucerne had caught my eye, but they and the city they overlook and defend, appeared more beautiful and exceedingly picturesque as I approached them by water from Weggis. The old wall, of which the gates and towers are still remaining, surrounds the land side of the town, which stands on a side hill rising gradually from the water; and all outside of the wall the hill is dotted with handsome dwellings embosomed in orchards and rich meadow lands; a picture of quiet beauty and a spot for classic repose that a weary man might almost be pardoned for coveting. The town itself has no pretensions to taste in its architecture, but for beauty of situation on the most attractive of all the Swiss lakes, it is without a rival. The hotels are on the borders of the lake at the very landing, and the lofty Pilatus on the right, the Rigi on the left, and the far loftier and more majestic heights of the Alps in the cantons of Schwytz and Uri are lying in full view of the *Swan* Hotel, where I lodged, a capital house, which I cordially commend.

We have been exploring the town to find what of interest may be in it, though it is scarcely worth while for any man to look down for a moment while he is in Switzerland, unless he is on the top of a hill. But Lucerne has one peculiar feature of interest, in its covered bridges adorned with curious paintings. In Berlin a gallery for the fine arts was opened over a stable, and some poet ridiculed the idea by suggesting the inscription " Musis et mulis," to the Muses and mules ; but the Lucerne people had the singular fancy of making their bridges over the River Reuss, which divides their town in two, the repository of paintings, some of them possessed of no artistic merit, and all of them more or less injured now by the weather. The bridges are roofed, and under the roof, about ten feet apart, these pictures in triangular frames are fastened up, so that the foot passenger, (no carriages are allowed,) may study them as he walks along. One series illustrates scenes in Swiss history—another on the reverse of the same canvass, the exploits of the patron saints of the town. These are on the Kapell-Bridge which starts near the Swan Hotel, and runs across the very rapid river Reuss, which here emerges from the lake. The Mill-bridge, lower down the river, has a very rude imitation of the paintings of the "Dance of Death," a series of pictures that are so often attempted, we may be sure they once had power on the minds of men. The originals are destroyed with the exception of the few fragments at Basle. The doggerel verse into which the German text is translated, is about equal in artistic excellence to the painting. The most remarkable bridge which Lucerne once boasted was across the end of the lake, but it has now been removed, the waters crowded back by the hand of art, and the large hotels now stand on the site of the old Hof-Bruche.

In the arsenal is a sacred deposit of old armor, and relics of more than doubtful authenticity, including the sword of William Tell, and the battle-axe which it is said the Reformer Zwingle carried in his hand on

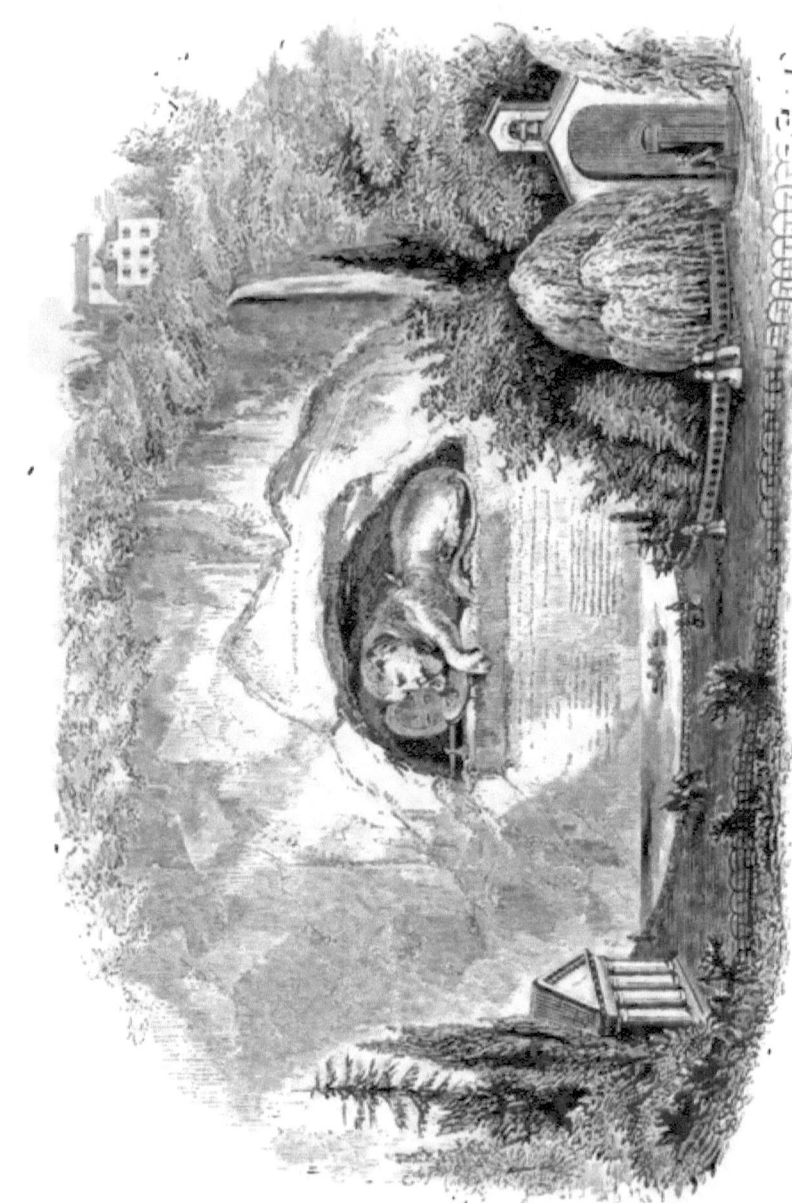

THE MONUMENT AT LUCERNE.

the field where he fell. A stranger may look at these and a hundred other curiosities, with some interest, if he has not been already surfeited, as I am, with the same sort of thing.

They have one lion here that *is* a lion—one of the noblest monuments and magnificent designs that I have seen in Europe. We passed through the Weggis Gate, and by a shaded pleasant walk in the private grounds of General Pfyffer, came to a lonely, lovely dell. On one side of it a huge precipice presents a bare rock face from which the water trickles into a little lake at the base. This rock is fringed on the sides and over the brow with shrubbery and trees, a graceful drapery, and in the solid side of the rock the figure of a dying lion is carved out of the same stone. A broken spear sticks in his side, and the blood oozes from the wound. The agony of death is in his face, but his paw rests on a shield with the arms of France, which even in death he is determined to defend. This monument was designed by the great Thorwalsden, but was executed by Ahorn, a sculptor of Constance, to commemorate the bravery of the Swiss guards who were slain at Paris while defending the Bourbons in the Revolution of 1792. This lion is nearly thirty feet long, and in just proportions, making an impressive monument better than the deed deserves. A representative of the Swiss guard wearing his uniform, is present to expound the design to those who are not quick at finding "sermons in stones."

A cool delightful walk of fifteen minutes from this sequestered spot brought us into the grounds of a little convent, pleasingly situated on the sloping banks, and among cultivated fields, now fragrant with new-mown hay. An aged priest came by, and taking off his hat politely saluted us as we passed. We paused at the door of the chapel; a single lamp was burning before the altar, and one lonely nun was on her knees performing her evening devotions. It was not in our hearts to disturb the calm current of her thoughts, as she was gazing on the picture of her Saviour, and we did not enter. So sweetly and gracefully did the villas lie among the green fields and fruit trees, with the lake in front of them and the snowy Alps on the other side of it, full in view, but far enough to be in another clime, that I felt very much like setting up a little convent there on a new plan, and sending over the sea, for the community to people it.

Aug. 24.—We had a storm on the Lake this evening. For two or three days the weather had been very hot, so much so that I was not disposed to go tramping, even for the sake of climbing up a hill into a colder atmosphere. We had been lying off, too lazy to write, or to read. So we went a fishing after dinner. The Apostles went fishing. They fished all night, and caught nothing: we fished all the afternoon and had the same success.

Just before nightfall, the wind began to blow all of a sudden as if it had broken out in a new place. It blew all ways at once. The little skiffs that were out on the Lake pulled in for shore with all haste; and in less time than I have taken to tell of it, the scene of calm beauty which the Lake had presented, was changed to that of an angry tempest-tossed sea. The whole valley was filled with black, fierce clouds. Rigi was clothed with thunder. Pilatus was totally obscured. The storm was coming from his quarter, confirming the superstition of the natives, that his troubled spirit stirs the tempest. Through a single break in the clouds I could see the sunshine playing among the valleys away to the south, while darkness and gloom were all around us. The contrast was striking and peculiar to this region, where the sudden elevation of the mountains makes the transitions from one temperature to another rapid. On the bosom of the Lake the reflections of the clouds were exceedingly curious, giving almost as many colors as the rainbow that now began to appear on the Rigi. It was a beautiful bow. No rain had yet fallen here; but there on the side of that noble mountain on whose summit I had spent the night, the blessed bow was resting; so pure, so glorious, so full of sweet suggestions of God's promise, that I looked on it as on the face of a friend in a strange land. It is just such a bow as they have in America. The same sun and the same showers make it, and the same God hangs it out there, the sign of his faithfulness, the token of his love. Who can be afraid of a storm when the rainbow appears? But it faded, as all bright things fade, and the dark clouds grew darker, and a heavy clap of thunder in the west shook the Alps, and another: not preceded by a streak of chain lightning leaping like a red serpent in the clouds, but by a broad lurid sheet of fire, filling the atmosphere, and then suddenly vanishing into darkness. The rain now came down in sheets; the wind blew with increasing power, and for a few moments it did indeed appear as if the prince of the powers of the air had been suffered to reign, and he was doing his worst while he was left unchained. The ignorance of the people could readily be imposed upon, when such scenes as this are frequent; and I am told, in former times so strictly was the ascent of Mount Pilatus forbidden, lest a storm should be provoked by the intrusion, that a Naturalist, Gessner, had to obtain a special license to pursue his investigations there.

The storm was of short duration. The hundreds,

induced by the clear bright morning to go to the
summit of Rigi for a sunset and a sunrise, found it
was not the entertainment to which they were
invited. In full view from my window, though five
hours distant, I can see where the clouds cap his
head, the rain is pouring there in torrents, the
western and eastern sky is enveloped in mists that
obscure all view of the sun, and more than half of
the time, there is as little to be seen from the summit
of Rigi, as in a cellar. The sun is shining brightly
now on the lake near me, and a great fleece, as if a
thousand flocks had yielded theirs for a robe, is thrown
over the crown of the mountain, making a veil that
no glass can see through.

The next morning we set off for a walk into the
country. The landlord of the Swan assured us it
would be a pleasant day, and as this prediction was
made at the risk of losing two guests in consequence,
we were bound to respect his judgment. We
resolved to make an expedition into the country
behind Lucerne, cross some of the spurs of the mountains, come around by the foot of old Pilatus, and so
return to our lodgings. The whole walk would be
only about twelve or fifteen miles, and if we should
lose our way and make it a little longer, why so
much the better.

It was just eight in the morning as we left and

wandered slowly through the streets with our Alpen-
stocks or pike staffs in hand. We paused at a church
door or two, and looked in, where a few were paying
their silent devotions before the altar, with a single
burning lamp, and passing out of the gate underneath
one of the seven old feudal towers, we took the bank
of the river Reuss, and walked by a pleasant path,
expecting every moment to find a bridge, as our road
was to lead us off to the west, and we must cross the
stream to reach it. I asked a little girl, tending two
babies in a cottage door, if there was any bridge in
that direction, and her ready answer "Nein," or *no*,
sent us about in a hurry. Here was the first mile
thrown away, and retracing our steps, we crossed at
the bridge near the wall, and taking the high road
toward Berne, were soon in the midst of rural Swiss
valley scenery. A path for a mile or more on the
bank of the river, shaded by a row of fine trees, led
along by the side of the carriage road, but we kept
the track, having little desire to miss it again.
Three miles of easy walking brought us past the
village of Lindau to a bridge over a deep and
frightful gorge, through which a mountain stream is
rushing, fifty or sixty feet below the bridge. Here it
is compressed in one place to a passage it has worn
for itself through the solid rock, and not more than
three feet wide, but the bed of the ravine gives

evidence that the torrent when swollen with melting
snows in early summer, or by heavy rains, may be
terrible, so that this massive bridge, though very
short, is required to resist its force. The sides of
this ravine were so precipitous that we did not
attempt the descent: but finding a path up the
mountain, and learning from a peasant whom we met
that it would take us over into a vale, we struck into
it, and climbed. The roots of trees in some places
made a flight of steps up which we walked, and all
the way it was so steep that to get on required
resolution and wind. But the ascent though sharp
was very short, and in a few minutes we reached a
well made winding way, that led us into a lovely
vale. Thirsty if not weary, we called at the door of
a little dwelling and asked for milk. The farmer
and his wife were sitting on wooden benches by a
table, taking their meal ; what meal it was we could
not determine, as it was ten o'clock in the morning ;
too late for breakfast, too early for dinner. They
had an earthen pot of weak coffee or something of
the same color, and pieces of brown bread which
they dipped in and ate, taking a drink of the fluid
now and then, and apparently enjoying their frugal
meal. The old woman gave me a " Yah" in answer
to my request for milk, and taking a glass tumbler
from a closet, she wiped the dust out of it with her

fingers, **and** going into a dark room, the **dairy likely,**
she brought **me a** draught **of as** sweet **milk** as ever
wet the lips **of man or boy.** The cottage was not
clean, I am sorry to say it. I looked up a flight of
stairs, and the appearance of things there did not
suggest to me the idea of taking lodgings, but giving
the woman a bit of silver for which she thanked me
in German, we walked on, refreshed with the milk
and the moment's-rest while getting it.

A little farther **on, and** a fine mansion **with castel-**
lated **towers,** stood on the rising hill commanding·a
wide prospect of mountain scenery, but the road **did**
not lead us near to it. Perhaps the proprietor of the
valley has his home up there, and the tenants below
may not be thriving : certainly it looks as if wealth,
state, comfort, and elegance were in those old halls,
and having had milk in the cottage, I presume we
might have wine in the mansion.

We soon lost sight of every sign of a dwelling, and
walked on through a pine forest, the saddest of all
forests to tread in : the sighing of the air through the
tree tops making a music " mournful to the soul." A
water course, in hollowed logs carried through the
woods, led on to a mill by the way-side, into which
we entered to see a novel operation, and as queer a
little miller as any body ever saw. The water turned
an overshot wheel outside of the mill, and this turned

two large wooden cog wheels, which raised two
beams and let them fall, up and down, upon pine
bark, which was thus pounded up fine enough to be
used for tanning. But the miller who fed the mill
with the bark was a man dwarf about three feet high,
well enough proportioned, a stout healthy fellow,
forty years old. He looked up and laughed us a
good morning, and went on with his work, which
made such a noise that it was useless to converse.
And just as we left the mill we met a woman not
more than three feet long, so nearly the same age and
size, we could not but think they might be another
remarkable pair of twins, who would have made the
fortune of any body bringing them to America for
exhibition.

We were now in a manufacturing valley. The fine
water power was improved to drive looms in a mill
where twenty girls were weaving, and when we
passed, which was at eleven o'clock, they all quit
for dinner, and trooped by us in rows of six abreast:
hearty looking girls with no hats on, their hair braided, and hanging in two strips half way to their feet.
They seemed to be very happy among themselves, and
modest and well behaved as we walked along with
them for a while. Other establishments for working
iron were in the same neighborhood, and a village
called *Kriens*, had some beautiful houses in it—one

of them with twelve windows in a row in front, and three stories high, a fine mansion; and all of them were surrounded with flower gardens, tended with care, and glowing with splendid dahlias, and other flowers. The best houses I have yet seen in Switzerland are covered instead of clapboards, with small, round-end shingles, put on so neatly as to look like scollop shell work. So we walked from one to another hamlet, studying life in these secluded places, where the habits of the people are quite as unsophisticated as if they had never been a mile from home—the children did not know of such a place as Lucerne, though not five miles off—but there was peace, order, thrift, and contentment—the mountains rise suddenly from behind their dwellings, and shelter them from the winds, and God watches them in the winter when the deep snow fills this vale, and they are as contented as if they knew that people live on the other side of the hills. Some of the cottages were beautifully covered with grape vines, trained between the windows, and giving them an appearance of luxurious growth, that might be adopted in our country far more than it is. The vine thus cultivated occupies no space that could otherwise be used, and is an ornament and protection, while it yields delicious and abundant fruit.

Our walk this morning of five hours brought us through this valley and back to Lucerne by one o'clock, and if there had been any good reason for it, we could have done a dozen miles more toward night. We had been brought more immediately into contact with the country people, and saw more of their way of life, than we would in a month of travel on the thoroughfares. None of the places we visited are even named in the guide books, and we thus had the pleasure of breaking out of the beaten path, and finding one that was new and interesting.

Lake of the Four Forest Cantons.

Lake Lucerne is called the Lake of the Four Forest Cantons, a longer but a very appropriate name, as its shores are washed by four and only four of the Cantons of Switzerland—Lucerne, Uri, Unterwalden, and Schwytz. Above all the lakes of the country, and perhaps of the world, it is distinguished for the majesty of its scenery and the grandeur of its historical associations.

Speaking of the classic history of the lake and mountains around it, Sir James McIntosh says :

" It is upon this that the superiority of the lake of Lucerne to all other lakes, or as far as I know, to all other scenes upon earth, depends. The vast mountains rising on every side, and closing at the end, with their rich clothing of wood, the soft spots of verdant pasture scattered at their feet, and some-

times on their breast, and the expanse of water
unbroken by islands, and almost undisturbed by any
signs of living men, make an impression which it
would be foolish to attempt to convey by words.
The only memorials which would not disgrace such a
scene as those of past ages renowned for heroism and
virtue, and no part of the world is more full of such
venerable ones."

The shores of this lake are the scenes of William
Tell's illustrious deeds, and the theatre also of
modern deeds of valor not surpassed by those of
ancient times. It was the contemplation of the
moral as well as the physical sublime in this region,
that led the same elegant author to write:

"The combination of whatever is grandest in
nature, with whatever is pure and sublime in human
conduct, affected me more powerfully in the passage
of this lake, than any scene which I had ever seen.
Perhaps neither Greece nor Rome would have had
such power over me. They are dead. The present
inhabitants are a new race who regard with little or
no feeling the memorials of former ages. This is
perhaps the only place in our globe where deeds of
pure virtue, ancient enough to be venerable, are
consecrated by the religion of the people, and
continue to command interest and reverence. No

local superstition so beautiful and so moral anywhere exists. The inhabitants of Thermopylae or Marathon know no more of those famous spots than that they are so many square feet of earth. England is too extensive a country to make Runnymede an object of national affection. In countries of industry and wealth the stream of events sweeps away these old remembrances. The solitude of the Alps is a sanctuary destined for the monuments of ancient virtue; Grutli and Tell's chapel are as much reverenced by the Alpine peasants as Mecca by a devout Musselman; and the deputies of the three ancient cantons met, so late as 1715, to renew their allegiance and their oaths of eternal union."

Filled with such emotions as these and fresh from the perusal of these fine passages I left Lucerne on a lovely morning in August, the atmosphere pleasantly cooled by the previous storms, and now a glorious cloudless sky hanging over this mountain sea. On a little island, and strange to say the only island in the lake, a monument of wood once stood to the memory of William Tell, but it was struck by lightning and has disappeared. Near it the bay of Kussnacht sets up, where is a chapel to mark the spot on which the arrow from Tell's unerring bow drank the heart's blood of his enemy and tyrant

4

Gessler; and a ruined castle said to have been
the prison to which Tell was destined when he made
his memorable escape of which we shall soon speak.
But the boat put up into another bay on the other
side under old Pilatus and landed passengers who
were taken into the small boats which ply continually among these bays, and distribute the passengers
at the several points from which they would make
their excursions into the country. Pilatus rises in
gloomy grandeur from the very shores of the water,
and its bifurcated peak soon is lost sight of, while but
one presents itself. Rugged, barren and uninviting
as it is, there are those who yet make the ascent, and
from this landing, though the ascent is far more
difficult, and the view from the summit far less
satisfactory than the Rigi.

We now returned to Kussnacht bay ; and if the
great shooting match which occurred last Monday
had been coming off to-day, we would go ashore to
see it. Once a year the marksmen of the canton
assemble for a trial of their skill with the rifle, and
there is also an annual festival, when the best from
all the cantons assemble for the federal shooting
match. With music and banners and processions,
with garlands and arches of victory and feasting and
drinking, they keep up this custom from generation
to generation ; and the riflemen of the Swiss and

Tyrol mountains, like their ancestors of the bow, have
no rival. The military displays were very miserable.
Having just come from France, Prussia, and Austria,
where the army was evidently the pet of govern-
ments, and the curse of the people, I was pleased to see
that the Swiss had no need of armies, and the military
procession was sorry enough. But the music was
stirring, and the Swiss feel it a part and parcel of
their patrimonial inheritance, to be roused by its
strains to noble deeds, or melted to tenderness by its
subduing power. The lake had assumed to the eye,
when looking down upon it from one slope of the
Rigi, the form of an X, and now the two promon-
tories that divide it come within a mile of each other,
and are called the Noses, which we pass, and enter
the bay of Brochs, where the Horn of that name and
Stawzer rear their lofty heads. We touched at
Bechenried, and then swept the width of the lake
again to *Gersau*, a little cluster of houses at the foot
of a gently-receding hill, one of the most remarkable
spots of land in the whole world, in the fact that for
four hundred years the people of this village, shut out
from the rest of mankind by these mighty ramparts
of mountains, and having but three miles long and
two wide of territory, maintained an independent
democratic government of their own. The French
invasion of 1798 destroyed their freedom by uniting

them to the Canton Schwytz. The mountain-side is covered with orchards, in the midst of which neat cottages nestle sweetly. All the land they have has been washed down from the mountains, and it would not be strange if trees and cottages and people should one day be washed into the lake together. Such a calamity would carry off the old gallows, still standing, but which the government had no occasion to use during its independent existence. Here the scenery of the lake becomes in the highest degree sublime. We stop for a moment at Brunnen, where goods are deposited that are to go over the Alps by St. Gothard into Italy, and on one of the warehouses you see three men painted in bold colors, and their names affixed, the heroes who with Tell achieved the deliverance of Switzerland in 1315. On this spot the alliance was formed between the three cantons of Uri, Unterwalden and Schwytz. Now the vast mountains rise more perpendicularly from the lake : a solitary rock stands a few feet from the shore on the promontory opposite, and passing it we seem to be issuing into a new lake altogether. Away on the ledges, or table land on the heights, stands a little church, and a few dwellings are scattered around, but we lose sight of them, and are now in the midst of a solitude of water, mountain, snow and sky, the grandeur and sublimity of which it is equally impossible for me to exaggerate or describe. No road, not even a footpath can be made along the base of these rocky mountains that literally stand in the water, and thence rear their heads so far into the upper air that the fields of snow lie there in full view, forever whitening in the sun. A little recession from the shore gives lodgment for soil enough to make a secluded bosom in the hills; and this *oasis* is a sacred spot in Swiss history, for here in the dead of night, the three confederates met to form their plans to deliver their country from the Austrian yoke. This is Grutli, and every American who passes the spot will feel a sympathetic thrill of joy to look on the birth-place of a country's freedom. Nearly opposite to Grutli, the steamboat slackens its speed, and moves slowly and solemnly by a small chapel, with an open front, and filled with rude paintings of scenes in Swiss history. This chapel is to commemorate the spot where Tell leaped ashore from the boat in which the tyrant Gessler was conveying him from Altorf to his dungeon in Kussnacht. A storm came up with such fury that Gessler, being frightened, and his oarsmen failing, ordered the chains to be taken off from Tell, that he might guide the skiff ashore. He ran it to this rock, leaped ashore, and made his escape. Before the despot reached his castle, Tell had waylaid him and sent an arrow to his heart. This chapel was " built in 1388, by the Canton of Uri, only thirty-one years after Tell's death, and in the presence of one hundred and fourteen persons who had known the hero. Once a year, mass is said, and a sermon preached in the chapel to the inhabitants of these borders, who repair hither in boats, forming an aquatic procession."

We were at the head of the lake in a few minutes. I was willling that it should be extended for hours, but the little village of Fluellen was reached, and here we go ashore. The village stands in a marsh, which is formed at the entrance of the river Reuss into the lake, and in consequence the people are subject to goitre and cretinism, those terrible diseases so peculiar to this country. It is not desirable to stay here any longer than is necessary to get away; and there is nothing to attract the stranger. We took the first carriage we found, and rode on to *Altorf*. At the hotel two young women came out to receive us, as men waiters would do in another country. It was a novelty to be thus received, and giving a hand to each of the damsels I was assisted from the carriage and escorted into the house. One of them, a fine-looking girl of eighteen, in a picturesque and becoming dress, white spencer and short sleeves with a dark skirt and bracelets, insisted on taking my knapsack, which I declined giving up, and leaning

on my Alpen stock, I had so much of an argument
with her that the travellers formed a circle about us
and looked on. While dinner was preparing I
walked out to the open square in which that scene
was enacted which has been more famous than any
other in Swiss history. Here by this fountain was
the tree to which the son of William Tell was bound,
with the apple on his head, and at the other fountain
the father stood, to obey the infamous order of the
tyrant to shoot with his cross-bow the apple from the
head of his lovely boy. A statue of the father sur-
mounts the fountain. The old village has all the
signs of decay, and I found it difficult to believe that
here the crowd had gathered five hundred years ago
to behold that dreadful spectacle—here stood the
monster who had given the cruel order, here fell the
arrows from beneath the garment of Tell, which he
declared he designed for the tyrant if his arrow had
slain his son. I walked out of the village into the
narrow meadow under the brow of overhanging
mountains, and admired the industry that has ter-
raced the slopes and wrung all the support it would
yield from the soil. A row of targets was here, with
evidences that the people having long since laid aside
the cross bow, are now experts with the rifle : and as
this village is the capital of the canton of Uri, it is
the rallying place for those trials of skill in which

they take so much delight. The tree on which Gessler's hat was hung, with the command that the people should bow down to it, stood here till 1567, when it was removed and a stone erected in its place.

The valley of Schachen, which we enter on leaving Altorf, delighted me with the beauty of its meadows, in which the Swiss peasants were making hay under a burning sun, while the mountains rising from the edge of the fields were white with snow. The men and women at noon when we passed were resting from their toil, and lying around on the mown grass, the very picture of slow and easy hay-makers. We crossed a rapid stream foaming in its downward course, in which William Tell was drowned while nobly striving to save the life of a child; and a little further on we passed the village in which he was born. Thus in a single day which is not yet half gone, we have seen the various spots in Switzerland made classic by the deeds of William Tell and his compatriots, and the places where that illustrious though rustic hero was born, where he performed his great exploits, and where he perished in the midst of one not less noble than any other that sheds honor on his name. It was a great day to have passed through all these scenes, and I can say, without affectation that my solitary walk in that ruined town of Altorf moved me more than the contemplation of any battle field in Europe.

CHAPTER V.

PASS OF SAINT GOTHARD.

The Priest's Leap—The Devil's Bridge—Night on the Mountains—Storm—
Hospenthal—the Glaciers—a Lady in Distress—the Furca Pass—Glacier of
the Rhone—Heinrich and Nature—Heinrich asks after God—Scene in the
Hospice.

E ARE now on the great road
that leads over the Alps into
Italy by the famous Pass of
St. Gothard. The diligence to
Milan went off this morning
at nine o'clock, and had we
come on in the earliest boat
from Lucerne, we might have
been taken on as far as we
liked by that lumbering conveyance. A party of
students, seven from Germany, and two from Oxford
joined us, and we resolved to hire a carriage to
Amsteg, two hours onward, and there to begin the

(81)   4*

ascent and pedestrianism together. The ride to Amsteg was lively, but when we were set down at that village, with a walk of five hours before us, all the way up the mountains, I confess to a slight sinking at the heart; and my courage oozed out gradually at the end of my toes. At the inn of Altorf, a young German student attracted me by the gracefulness of his manner, the delicacy of his features, and the pleasant expression with which he conversed. He attached himself to our party, and we walked on together, pilgrims to see Switzerland, and rejoicing in the power to take leave of all modes of travelling, but that first and best, which nature had provided. The river Reuss comes dashing along down with the fury of a young torrent, pouring over rocks, and whirling around precipices with a madness that brooks no control. The Bristenock mountain towers aloft into the regions of snow and ice, and nature begins to grow wild and dreary. The soft meadows on which the maids of Uri were making hay have disappeared, and the green pastures with frequent herds are now the only hope of the shepherd. The road is no longer a straight path, but in its toilsome way upward, it crosses again and again this foaming river, and bridges of solid masonry, built to resist the flood when it bears the ruins of avalanches on its bosom, and spreads them in the spring on the plains below.

We crossed the third bridge and came to a gorge of frightful depth through which the river rages furiously, in a maddened torrent too fearful to look on without awe. It is called Pfaffensprung, or the Priest's Leap, from a story — which no one will believe who stands here—that a monk once leaped across the chasm with a maiden in his arms. I have no doubt a monk would do his best under the circumstances, but I doubt the possibility of his clearing thirty feet at a bound over such an abyss as this, even for the sake of the prize he is said to have carried off. We had been beset by beggars under all sorts of guises, and here a miserable old woman—alas that a woman could come to this— appeared with a huge stone in her hands, which she hurled into the deeps, for us to see it leap from rock to rock and finally sink into the raging waters far below. A few cents she expected for this service, and she received them with gratitude; when an old man, perhaps her husband, came on with another rock which he was willing to drop for a similar consideration. As I turned away from the scene, a carriage came up in which an English gentleman was riding, with two servants on the box. I walked by the side of his carriage and fell into conversation,

when he very politely invited me to ride with him.
I declined of course, and told him that I was making
a pedestrian tour, and designed to walk to Andermatt, three hours and a half farther up the mountain.
"I spend the night there also," he said, " and I will
esteem it an honor, Sir, if you will take a seat in my
carriage." Such an invitation, under the circumstances, was not to be refused, and I took a seat by
the gentleman's side. How wonderfully the scenery
improved, certainly how much my appreciation of it
increased, when I fell back on the cushions! My
companion was an accomplished member of the London bar. He knew public men whom I had met, and
was well acquainted with all subjects of international
interest, so that in fifteen minutes we were comparing
minds on those questions in which England and
America are so much concerned. We stopped at the
little village of Wasen for refreshments. I insisted on
paying the reckoning, when he stopped me with this
remark, " Sir, you are my guest to-day : when I
meet you in America I shall be happy to be yours."

We rode on and upward, the road now assuming
the character of a mighty structure of masonwork
through a savage defile, only wide enough for the
carriage-path, and the torrent of the Reuss, which no
longer flows, but tumbles headlong from one cliff to
another, while for three or four miles the lofty preci-

pices hang fearfully on high. In the spring, the rage
of this mountain river, swollen by melting snows, and
bringing down ice and rocks in its thundering fall,
would tear away the foundations of any common
pathway, and this must be built to defy the fiercest
storm. Twenty-five or thirty thousand persons cross
the Alps by this route every year; and to secure this
travel, which would otherwise be carried off to the
other passes, the cantons of Uri and Tessin built a
road which has twice been swept away by the avalanches, but one would think that the present might
stand while the mountains stand. So rapid is the
ascent, that the road is made often to double on itself,
so that we are going directly backward on the route;
a foot passenger may clamber across the doublets and
save his time, but the carriage must keep the zig-zag
way, patiently toiling up a smoother and more beautiful highway than can be found in the most level
region of the United States of America! Not a
pebble in the path: the wheels meet no other
obstruction than gravitation, which is sufficient to
be overcome only by the strongest of horse power.
Yet through this very defile, long before any road
like this had been built, three armies, the French and
the Russians and the Austrians, have pursued each
other, contesting every inch of this ground, and each
one of these rugged heights, and disputing the posses-

sion of dizzy cliffs where the hunter was afraid to
tread. Never did the feeling of Nature's awful wildness so take possession of my soul, as when night was
shutting in upon me in this dreary pass. Sometimes
the road is hewn out of the solid rock in the side of
the precipice, which hangs over it as a roof, and
again it is borne over the roaring stream, which in a
gulf four hundred feet below is boiling in its
obstructed course, and making for itself an opening,
it leaps away over the rocks, and rushes down while
we are toiling up. In the day-time it would be
gloomy here; it will be terrible indeed if the darkness overtakes us before we reach our resting-place
for the night.

More than five hundred years ago an old Abbot of
Einsiedeln built a bridge over an awful chasm here,
but such is the fury of the descending stream, the
horrid ruggedness of the surrounding scenery, the
smoothness and solidity of the impending rocks, the
roar and rage of the waters as they are tossed about
and beaten into spray, and so unlikely does it appear that human power could ever have reared a
bridge over such a cataract, that it has been called
from time immemorial the Devil's Bridge, and so it
will be called probably till the end of time. It was
just nightfall when we reached it. It was very cold,
so far up had we ascended. We had left the carriage

THE DEVIL'S BRIDGE.

and were walking to quicken the blood, when the roar of the waters rose suddenly upon us, the spray swept over us, and we were in the midst of a scene of such awful grandeur, and with terror mingled, as might well make the nerves of a strong man tremble. The river Reuss, at this stage of its course, makes a sweeping leap, a tremendous plunge at the very moment it bends nearly in a semi-circle, while the rocks, as if by some superhuman energy, have been hurled into the torrent's path, so as to break its fall, but not to withstand its power. Two bridges are here— for when the old road was swept away, the bridge defied the storm, and this one, more solid and of far greater span, has been thrown high above the other which is left as an architectural curiosity in the depths below. And long before that was built, another one was there, and when the French in 1799 pursued the Austrians over it, and while the embattled hosts were making hell in a furious fight upon and over this frightful gorge, the bridge was blown up, and the struggling foes were whelmed together in the devouring flood. A month afterwards, and the Russians met the French at the same spot—no bridge was here, but the fierce Russians bound timbers together with the scarfs of the officers, threw them over the chasm, crossed in the midst of a murderous fire, and drove the enemy down the Pass into the vales below.

It was dark before we were willing to quit this fearful place. The strength of the present bridge is so obvious, and the parapet so high, that the scene may be contemplated without fear ; but the clouds had now gathered, hoarse thunder muttered among the mountains, spiteful squalls of rain, cold, gloomy, and piercing, were driving into our faces, and we were anxious to find shelter for the night. We left the Bridge, but in another moment plunged into utter darkness as we entered a tunnel called the *Hole of Uri*, where the road is bored one hundred and eighty feet through the solid rock, a hard but the only passage, as the stream usurps the rest of the way, and the precipice admits no possible path over its lofty head. This was made a hundred and fifty years ago, and before that time the passage was made on a shelf supported by chains let down from above. It was called the Gallery of Uri, and along it a single traveller could creep, if he had the nerve, in the midst of the roar and the spray of the torrent, and with an hungry gulph yawning wide below him.— Emerging from this den, we entered a valley five thousand feet above the sea ; once doubtless a lake, whence the waters of the Reuss have burst the barriers of these giant fortresses, and found their way into more hospitable climes. No corn grows here, but the land flows with milk and honey—by no means an indication of fertility, for the cows and the goats find pasture at the foot of the glaciers, and the bees their nests in the stunted trees and the holes of the rocks. We drove through it till we came to Andermatt, where the numerous lights in the windows guided us to a rustic tavern.

By this time it had commenced raining hard, and I began to be anxious for my young friend Rankin, and a German student, Heinrich. But I could do no more for them than to send a man to watch in the highway till they should come up, and lead them into the house where I was resolved to spend the night, whether we could find beds or not. These rural inns in Switzerland are rude and often far from comfortable. But travellers here must not stand upon trifles. The house was designed to lodge twenty travellers, and thirty at least were here before us. A large supper table was spread, and around it a company of gentlemen and ladies, mostly German, were enjoying themselves right heartily, after the day's fatigue was over. The London lawyer and myself had a separate table laid for us—we soon gathered on it some of the good things of this life, which by the way you can find almost every where, and had made some progress in the discussion of the various subjects before

us, when Rankin and Heinrich arrived nearly exhausted with their toilsome walk. They had a dreadful tale to tell of the storm they had met—which we
just escaped, and barely that. The lightning filled
the gloomy gorge, lighting up for an instant the
mighty cliffs and hanging precipices, while the thunder roared above the sound of the torrent, and the
rain drove into their faces, disputing with them the
upward pass. But they were young men, and strong.
They told me that I never could have borne the labor
and the exposure of the walk. Two travellers and a
guide had given out, and taken lodgings in a hamlet
we had passed, and the man whom we had employed
to bring on our light bags, had also halted for the
night, and would come up early in the morning.

After supper I led them to our chamber. Upon
my arrival, the landlady assured me that every bed
in the house was full, but I insisted so strenuously on
having *three*, that the girls exchanged looks of
agreement, and one of them offered to show me a
chamber, if it would be acceptable. She led me up
three pair of stairs, into a low garret bed-room, with
one window of boards which could be opened, and
one small one of glass that could not, and here were
three beds kindly given up by the young women.
Into this chamber I now conducted my young
friends.

Worn out with their hard day's work, but free from all anxious care, they were asleep in five minutes, while I coaxed the candle to burn as long as it would, fastened it up with a pin on the top of the candlestick, and tried to write the records of the few past hours. It was amusing to hear my companions, one on each side of me, talk in their sleep; Heinrich in his native German, and Rankin in his English, showing the restlessness of over-fatigue, while I sat wondering at myself, so lately a poor invalid, now in this wild region, exposed to such nights of discomfort, and days of toil. Yet was I grateful even there, not only for a safe shelter and a much better bed than my Master had, but for the strength to attempt such things, and for the luxury of health that lives and flows in a genial current through every part of a renovated frame.

In the morning I met an American gentleman returning from the summit of St. Gothard pass, and he advised me strenuously not to go further up, unless I was going now into Italy. The most wonderful of the engineering in the construction of the road, had already been seen, and there was nothing else of interest above. The same savage scenery, in the midst of which the Reuss leaps down 2,000 feet in the course of a two hours' walk, is continued, and the dreariness of desolation reigns alone.

A house for the accommodation of travellers has been maintained for hundreds of years, destroyed at times and then restored, and a few monks have been supported here to extend what aid they may to those who require their assistance. We resolved to pursue a route through the *Furca* pass, one of the most romantic and interesting of all the passes in Switzerland. A long day's walk it would be over frozen mountains and by the side of never melting glaciers, and no carriage way! Nothing but a bridle and a foot path, and a rough one too, was now before us, and if we left the present road, and struck off over the Furca, it would be four or five days before we should reach the routes which are traversed by wheels. Our baggage, though but a bag apiece and blankets, was too heavy for us to carry if we walked, and I proposed to take a horse, put on him our three bundles, and ride by turns. Heinrich had never heard of the mode of travelling called "ride and tie," and he was greatly amused when it was described to him. Accordingly we ordered a horse for the day. The price is regulated by law, under the pretence of protecting the traveller, but really for the purpose of extorting from him a sum twice as large as he would have to pay if the business were open to competition. The horse was brought to the door, and when we ordered the bags of three to be strapped on, the landlord flew into a great rage, and declared he would not be imposed upon. I smiled in his red face, and asked, " If he knew how much baggage the law allowed each man to carry on his horse." He said he did, and I then told him to weigh those, and he might have for his own all over and above the legal allowance. He was still dissatisfied, but when we bade him to take his old nag to the stable, he suddenly cooled. Without further delay he made fast " the traps," gave me a good stout fellow to conduct the party and bring back the beast. An idle group of guides and tavern hangers, and quite a party of Germans and English were looking on when I bestrode the animal, and took my seat in the midst of the bundles rising before and behind, like the humps of a camel. We are yet in the vale of the Urseren, not more than a mile wide, and lofty mountains flanking its sides. The mountain of St. Anne is clad with a glacier, from which the " thunderbolts of snow" come down with terrific power in the spring, and yet there stands a forest in the form of a triangle, pointing upward, and so placed that the slides of snow as they come down are broken in pieces and guided away from the village below. The great business of the people in this vale is to keep cattle and to fleece the strangers who travel in throngs over the pass of St. Gothard. Hundreds of horses are kept for hire, and nothing is to be had by a "foreigner" unless he pays an exorbitant price. Even the specimens of minerals are held so high, that no reasonable man can afford to buy them. But we are now leaving Andermatt, and on the side of the road not long after leaving the village we saw two stone pillars, which need but a beam to be laid across them, and they make a gallows, on which criminals were formerly hung, when this little valley, like Gersau on the lake, was an independent state. The pillars are still preserved with care, as a memorial of the former sovereignty of the community.

We reached *Hospenthal* in a few moments; a cluster of houses about a church, and with a tower above the hamlet which is attributed to the Lombards. I was struck with the exceeding loneliness and forsakenness of this spot. It seemed that men had once been here, but had retired from so wild and barren a land, to some more genial clime. Hospenthal has a hotel or two, and it is a great halting place for travellers who are about to take our route over the Furca to the Hospice of the Grimsel. Here we quit the St. Gothard road, and winding off by a narrow path in which we can go only in single file, we are soon out of the vale, and slowly making our way up the mountain. The hill sides are dotted with the huts of the poor peasants, who have hard work to hold fast to the slopes with one hand, while they work for a miserable living with the other. The morning sun was playing on the blue glacier of St. Anne, and a beautiful waterfall wandered and tumbled down the mountain; yet this was but one of many of the same kind that we are constantly meeting as we go through these defiles of the high Alps. The vast masses of snow and ice on the summits are sending down streams through the Summer, and these sometimes leap from rock to rock, and again they clear hundreds of feet at a single bound; slender, like a long white scarf on the green hill, but very picturesque and beautiful. At the foot of this mountain are the remains of an awful avalanche, which buried a little hamlet here in a sudden grave, and a sad story of a maiden and a babe who perished, was told me with much feeling by the guide as we passed over the spot. The peasant men and women were bringing down bundles of hay on their heads and shoulders from the scanty meadows which here and there in a warm bosom of the hills may be found, and as they descended I recalled the story of Orpheus, at whose music the trees are said to have followed him, and I could readily understand that such a procession might be taken or mistaken for the marching of a young forest.

5

We are still following up the river Reuss towards its
source, and though it is narrower, it is often fiercer
and makes longer strides at a step than it did last
evening.   We cross it now and then on occasional
stones, or on rude logs, and come to a spot where the
bridge was swept away last night by an avalanche of
earth and ice, and well for us that it came in the
night before we were here to be caught.   An old
man with a pickaxe in his hand had been working to
repair the crossing, and had managed to get a few
stones arranged so that foot passengers could leap
over, and the horses after slight hesitation and careful
sounding of the bottom, took to the torrent and waded
safely over. · I held my feet high enough to escape a
wetting, but I heard a lady of another party com-
plaining bitterly that the water was so deep or her
foot so far down, I could not tell which, but it was
evident that very much against her will she had been
·drawn through the river.

At Realp, a little handful of houses, we found a
small house of refreshment, where two Capuchin
friars reside to minister to travellers, and this was
the last sign of a human habitation we saw for some
weary hours.   We are now so far up in the world,
that the snow lay in banks by the side of the path,
while flowers, bright beautiful flowers were blooming
in the sun.   It is difficult to reconcile this apparent

contradiction in nature. The fact is not surprising here, where we see such vast accumulations of snow and remember that a short summer does not suffice to melt it, but it is strange to read of flowery banks all gay and smiling, within a few feet only of these heaps of snow. I counted flowers of seven distinct colors, and gathered those that would press well in my books, souvenirs of this remarkable region. On the right the Galenstock Glacier now appears, and out of it vast rocks like the battlements of some old castle shoot 1,000 feet into the air. I am now among the ice palaces of the earth. The cold winds are sweeping down upon me, and I hug my coat closer as the ice blast strikes a chill to my heart.

We were just making the last sharp ascent before reaching the summit of the Furca when I overtook a lady sitting disconsolately by the wayside. She cried out as soon as I came up, "O Sir, my guide is such a brute—the saddle turns under me and I cannot get him to fix it—my husband has gone on before me—I cannot speak a word of German and the dumb fool cannot speak a word of English. What shall I do?"

"Madam," said I, "my servant shall arrange your saddle, and I will conduct you to the summit where the rest of your party will doubtless wait." She overpowered me with her expressions of gratitude, and while my servant was putting her saddle girths to rights, I gave her guide the needful cautions, and we crossed a vast snow bank together, climbed the steep pitch, and in ten minutes reached the inn at the top of the Furca. Distant glaciers, snow clad summits, ridges, and ranges stood around me, a world without inhabitants, desolate, cold and grand in its icy canopy and hoary robes of snow.

The descent was too rapid and severe for riding, and giving the horse into the charge of the servant we walked down, discoursing by the way of things rarely talked of in the Alps. My young German friend had all the enthusiasm of the French charact   joined to the mysticism of his own nation. He is well read in English literature, and familiar with ancient and modern authors, so that we had sources unfailing, to entertain us as we wandered on ; now sitting down to rest and now bracing ourselves for a smart walk over a rugged pass. I became intensely interested in him, though I had constant occasion to challenge his opinions, and especially to contrast his philosophy with the revealed wisdom of God. We had spoken of these things for an hour or more when I asked him if he had ever read " the Pilgrim's Progress," and when I found he had not, I told him the design of the allegory, and said " we are pilgrims over these mountains, and have been cheering one another with pleasing discourse as the travellers did on their way to the celestial city. They came at last in sight of its gates of pearl."

" But what is that ?"

We had suddenly turned the shoulder of a hill, and a glacier of such splendor and extent burst upon our view as to fix us to the spot in silent but excited admiration. It was the first we had seen near us. Others had been lying away in the far heights, their surface smoothed by the distance, and their color a dull blue ; but now we were at the foot of a mountain of ice ! We could stand upon it, walk on its face, gaze on its form and features, wonder, admire, look above it and adore ! This is the glacier of the Rhone ! That great river springs from its bosom, first with a strong bound as if suddenly summoned into being, works its way through a mighty cavern of ice, and then winds along the base till it emerges in a roaring, milky white stream and rushes down the valley toward the sea. This glacier has been called a " magnificent sea of ice." It is not so. That description conveys no idea of the stupendous scene. You have stood in front of the *American* fall of Niagara. Extend that fall far up the rapids, receding as it rises a thousand feet or more from where you stand to the crest : at each side of it let a tall mountain rise as a giant frame work on which the tableau is to rest; then suddenly congeal this cataract, with its curling

waves, its clouds of spray, its falling showers of
jewelry, point its brow with pinnacles of ice, and
then, then let the bright sun pour on it his beams,
giving the brilliancy not of snow but of polished ice
to the vast hill-side now before you, and you will
then have but a faint conception of the grandeur of
this glacier.

"It answers," said Heinrich, "to Burke's definition
of the sublime—it is vast, mysterious, terrible!"

I replied that "it was impossible for me to have
the sensation of fear, and scarcely of awe in looking
upon the scene before us—it rather had to me the
image of the outer walls of heaven, as if there must
be infinite glory within and beyond when such majesty and beauty were without. And then these flowers
skirting the borders of this frozen pile, and smiling as
lovely as beneath the sunniest slope in Italy, forbade
the idea that this crystal mountain was of ice."

"But will it not vanish if we look away?" said
Heinrich, as he gazed on the frozen cataracts, and
gave utterance to his admiration in the most express-
ive words that German, French, English, Latin or
Greek would supply, for our discourse was in a mixture of them all.

Soon after passing the Glacier of the Rhone we met
a peasant who assured us that he had fallen into one
of its crevices, seventy feet, and had cut his way up

with a hatchet, thus delivering himself from an icy
grave.

A little wayside inn gave us a brief respite from
our toilsome journey. We climbed the Grimsel, and
reached the Dead Sea on its summit. It is called the
Lake of the Dead, because the bodies of those who
perished in making this journey were formerly cast
into it for burial. Heinrich and I left the path and
climbed to a cliff where we looked down on the pilgrim parties on horses and on foot, winding their way
along its borders. We sent our servant onward to
engage beds for us at the hospice of the Grimsel, and
resolved to spend the rest of the day (the sun was yet
three hours high) in this wilderness of mountain scenery.

We could now look down into the valley, a little
valley, but like an immense cauldron, the sides of
which are sterile naked rocks, eight hundred feet
high! On the west they stand like the walls and
towers of a fortified city, and in the bottom of the
vale is a single house and a small lake; but a flock
of a hundred goats and a score of cows, with tinkling
bells, are picking a scanty subsistence among the
stones. The scene was wild, savage, grand indeed,
and had there been no sun to light it up with the
lustre of heaven, it would have been dreary and dismal. Heinrich had been very thoughtful for an hour.

He had discovered that my thoughts turned constantly to the God who made all these mountains, while he was ever studying the mountains themselves.

" Here I will commune with nature."

I replied, " And I will go on a little further, and commune with God!"

" Stay," he cried, " I would go with you."

" But you cannot see Him," I said—" I see Him in the mountain and the glacier and the flower: I hear Him in the torrent and the still small voice of the rills and little waterfalls that are warbling ever in our ears. I feel his presence and something of his power. I beg you to stay and commune with nature, while I go and commune with God."

I left him and wandered off alone, and in an hour went down the mountain, and to my chamber in the hospice. I was sitting on the bedside, arranging the flowers I had gathered during the day, when Heinrich entered, and giving me his hand said to me, " I wish you would speak more to me of God!"

He sat down by my side, and I asked him if he believed the Bible to be the Word of God.

He said he did, but he would examine it by the light of history and reason, and reject what he did not find to be true.

" And do you believe that the soul of man will live hereafter?"

"I doubt," was his desponding answer.

I then addressed him tenderly, "My dear young friend, I have loved you since the hour I met you at Altorf. And now tell me, with all your studies have you yet learned how to die? You *doubt*, but are you so well satisfied with your philosophy that you are able to look upon death among the mountains, or by the lightning, without fear? My faith tells me that when I die my life and joy will just begin, and go on in glory forever. This is the source of all my hopes, and it gives me comfort now when I think that I may never see my native land and those I love on earth again. I *know* that in another land we shall meet?"

"How do you know that you shall meet?"

"My faith, my heart, my Bible tells me so. I shall meet all the *good* in heaven. I am sure of one child, an angel now."

"And where are your children?"

"Four in America, and one in heaven. I had a boy four years ago; earth never had a fairer. His locks were of gold and hung in rich curls on a neck and shoulders whiter than the snow: his brow was high and broad like an infant cherub's; and his eye was blue as the evening sky. And he was lovelier than he was fair. But in the budding of his beauty, he fell sick and died."

5*

"O no, not died!"

"Yes, he died here by my heart. And that child is the only one of mine that I am sure of ever seeing again."

"I do not understand you."

"If my other children grow up to *doubt* as *you* doubt, they may wander away on the mountains of error or the glaciers of vice, and fall into some awful gulph and be lost forever. And if I do not live to see my living children, I am as sure of meeting that one now in heaven, as if I saw him here in the light of the setting sun.—Heinrich, have you a mother, my dear friend?"

"Yes, yes," he cried, "and her faith is the same as yours."

I had seen his eyes filling, and had felt my own lips quivering as I spoke, but now he burst into tears and fell on my breast. He kissed my lips, and my cheeks, and my forehead, and the hot tears rained on my face, and mingled with my own. "O teach me the way to feel and believe," he said at last, as he clung to me like a frightened child, and clasped me convulsively to his heart. I held him long and tenderly, and felt for him somewhat, I hope, as Jesus did for the young man who came to him with a similar inquiry. *I loved him*, and longed to lead him to the light of day.

CHAPTER VI.

GLACIERS OF THE AAR.

My new Friend—a Wonderful Youth—Hospice of the Grimsel—the Valley—a comfortable Day—Glaciers of the Aar—a Gloomy Vale—Climbing a Hill—View of the Glacier—Theory of its Formation—Caverns in the Ice—Incidents of Men falling in—My Leap and Fall—an Artist Lost—Return.

EINRICH proved to be a wonderful youth. He had a warm heart, and his intellect was cultivated to a degree not parallelled in my acquaintance among young men. He was just one and twenty years of age, and had not completed the usual course of collegiate education. But there was no author in the Latin or Greek languages, poet, philosopher or historian, whose works I have ever heard of, which were not familiar to him, as the English Classics are to well read men in England or America. He discoursed readily of the

(107)

style, the dialect, the shade of sentiment on any disputed point; he cited passages and drew illustrations from the pages of ancient literature which seemed to him like household words: and one of our amusements when crossing the Alps was to discuss the difference in Greek or Latin words which are usually regarded as synonymes. But classical learning was the least and lowest attainment of this accomplished youth. The whole range of Natural Sciences had been pursued with a zeal that might be called a passion. Botany and Mineralogy were child's play to him: and Chemistry had been a favorite study evidently, for its principles often came up in our rambling discourse, and he was master of it as if he had been a teacher of the science for years. Geology was a hobby of his, and he thrust it upon me often when I wished he would let me alone, or discourse of something else. And yet when I have said all this I have not mentioned the department in which he was most at home, where his soul revelled in profound enjoyment, and in which he was resolved to spend his life. *Metaphysics* was his favorite pursuit. His analytical mind was always on the track of investigation, challenging a reason for everything, questioning the truth of every proposition, and never resting till his reason had subjected it to the most exhausting process. Yet in the midst of these studies including many departments to which I have not referred, as the exact sciences, he had polished this fine intellect by the widest course of polite literature, perusing in the German translations, all the old masters of the English tongue, admiring Shakespeare and Milton, quoting from them as a scholar would from Sophocles or Homer, and surprising me by reference to English authors, whose works I had not supposed were translated into the German language. Of course the poets and philosophers of his father-land were his pride and love. Often he would speak of them in terms of endearment, as if they were his personal friends; though of all beings, present or past, in heaven or out of it, I think he loved Plato most. This boy was just out of his teens, a student still, and modest as he was learned; burning to learn more; asking questions till it was tiresome to hear them; and never dreaming that he knew more than others. He was the most learned young man I ever saw. And few old men know half as much. He now joined my party, leaving his own altogether, and resolved to follow me to the ends of the earth.

We are now in the Vale of the Grimsel. In the bottom of the Valley, by the side of a lake forever dark with the shadows of overhanging hills, is the *Hospice*, a name that here combines the idea of hospital and hotel—its design being to furnish lodging and entertainment to travellers, whether they are able to pay for the hospitality or not. Last winter the landlord of the Grimsel having insured his house, set fire to it, to get the money, and now is in prison for twenty years as the penalty of his crime. In years past there have been terrible avalanches here, and once the house was crushed by the " thunderbolts of snow." Often it is surrounded by snow drifts twenty or thirty feet high, yet some one lodges here all winter to keep up a fire and furnish shelter to the benighted traveller. It is strange that these lonely paths should be traversed at all in the depth of winter. But there is no other mode of communication between the valleys, than along these defiles, and the traffic among the people of one canton with another is carried on, and the intercourse of families is kept up at the risk of life here as in other countries. If one has a good home, it were better to stay in it than to cross the Grimsel in the winter.

A mixed multitude were under the roof of the Hospice. The building is yet unfinished; and it must have required prodigious exertions to get it so far under way, since the fire, as to make it habitable for travellers this season. Every stick of timber must be brought up by hand from the plain some miles below. The walls are of stone, about three feet thick, and rough enough. No attempt to smooth a wall, or paint a board appears on the edifice, and the rude bedsteads, benches and chairs suggest to the luxurious traveller how few of the good things he has at home are actually essential to his comfort. The house has about forty beds, but these were far from being sufficient to give each weary pilgrim one. Many were obliged to choose the softest boards in the dining room floor, and sleep on them. Yet in that company of sixty who crowded around the supper table were many of the learned, and titled, and beautiful, and wealthy of many lands; meeting socially in a dreary valley, on a journey of pleasure, and refreshing each other with the "feast of reason and the flow of soul." Reserve was banished, and the hour freely given to good cheer, in which all strove to forget the toils of the day, in the pleasures of the evening, and the repose of a peaceful night.

Within an hour's walk from the door of the Hospice is the Glacier of the Aar, the most interesting and instructive of all the Glaciers of Switzerland. It has been more studied by men of science than any other. Agazziz and Forbes had their huts on its bosom, and spent many long and weary months in prying into the mysteries of these stupendous seas of solid water. Not one of the whole company who staid at the Hospice last night, turned aside for a day to study with us this wonderful scene. A party of

English people read the guide book on the route to
Meyringen, and congratulated themselves on having
a "comfortable" day, as there was very little to see!
They were *doing* Switzerland, and were evidently
pleased to find a day before them when they had
nothing to do but to go on, without being worried
with fine views and climbing hills. One party after
another came down and took a wretched cup of
coffee, and were off on their pilgrimage, some on
foot, some on mules, and one or two were carried on
chairs by porters.

We were left alone at the Hospice, and after
breakfast set off to spend the day on the Glaciers.
There are two of them, the Obi and Unter, or Upper
and Lower; the latter being the most easily reached,
and happily the most interesting. It is eighteen
miles long, and about three miles wide. To circum-
navigate it therefore, is not the journey of a day, but
it may be explored on foot, and Hugi, the naturalist,
is said to have rode over it on a horse. The morning was not promising. Heavy mists had lodged in
the vale of the Grimsel. But far above them in
gloomy grandeur rose the sterile ridges of rocks,
towering aloft, and looking like the battlements of
giants' castles, inaccessible save to the chamois and
his pursuer, who often risked, and sometimes threw
away his life in his daring adventures to secure his

prey. Even the chamois has now almost entirely disappeared, and the eagles alone have their dwelling places in these desolate abodes. Yet from the lofty heights some beautiful cascades are pouring all the way down into the vale, foaming as they fall; and sometimes caught by the intervening rocks, and sent out from the side of the precipice they melt into spray, and again on a lower ledge are gathered to pursue their downward course. Along the bottom of this gloomy vale we walked for an hour, till we came in sight of a mighty pile of earth, rocks, ice and snow. At first we thought we had come to a vast heap of sand, or to the *debris* brought down by an avalanche of soil with stones intermingled, but from the base of it a torrent was rushing, not of clear blue water, but of a dirty milky hue, as are all the streams when they issue from the beds of these Glaciers. The front of the mass was perhaps one hundred and fifty feet high, and nearly perpendicular, and here it was half a mile in width. On nearer approach, we could see the rocks of blue ice projecting through the coating of earth, showing plainly that the body of the great pile before us was the cold icebergs hid beneath a covering of earth that had been washed down upon it, from the mountains above. Now and then large masses of earth, or a huge boulder would be dislodged from the brow of the pile, and thunder along down, as we sat watching for these miniature avalanches. The sense of the terrible was strong upon us now. It was not beautiful: it was grand and awful, as we changed our position lest the falling rocks should overtake us in their course. But a few little birds were flying about from stone to stone unconscious of danger, the solitary inhabitants of this frozen world.

We now determined to ascend and look on its face. With incredible toil we climbed the hill by the side of it. If there ever was a path, we could not find it, but from rock to rock, often pulling ourselves up by the stunted bushes, we worked our way. Onward and upward we mounted, and at last were rewarded for the struggle by standing abreast of the glacier, where we could walk around and upon it and contemplate its stupendous proportions. From the bosom of it rises the Finster-Aarhorn, a lone pyramid that seems now to touch the blue sky: so cold and stern it stands there, its head forever covered with snow and its foot in this everlasting ocean of ice. The Schreckhorn is the other peak that stands yet farther off, but the clouds are now so dense around its summit, that I cannot see its hoary head.

Here we are six thousand feet above the level of the sea, and for three-quarters of the year the snow is falling on these mountains: not an April snow that melts as it falls, but a dry powder, into

which a man without snow - shoes would sink
out of sight, as in the water. On the loftiest of these
mountains, the surface of the snow melts a little
every day, and the deeper you descend into the
snow, the melting is going on also. But at night it
freezes, as by day for a little while it thaws, and this
process is continued until the snow is gradually converted into ice. The high valleys are filled with
these ever increasing deposits of snow, which are
thus constantly undergoing this change, and as the
fresh deposit far exceeds what is carried off by melting, the enormous mass is rather increased than
diminished by the lapse of time. It becomes a fixed
fact; yet not fixed, for the most remarkable, and to
my mind, the sublimest fact in this relation, is that
these glaciers are actually moving steadily, year by
year. The projecting mass in the lowest valley, as
where we were standing a few hours ago, is melting
away, and sending out the river that leaves its bosom
on its mission into a world far below. Underneath
the glacier, where it presses on the earth, which has
a heart of fire, the work of dissolution is rapidly going
on, while the sun on the upper surface melts the ice,
and streams flow along and cut deep crevices into
which the uncautious traveller may fall never to rise
again till the last day. Some of these glaciers may
be traversed underneath, by following the streams.

Hugi wandered a mile in this way underneath magnificent domes, through which the sun-light was streaming, and among crystal columns which had been left standing as if to support the superincumbent mass. The water, as in rocky caverns, trickles through and freezes in beautiful stalactytes, to adorn these palaces, unseen except by the eye to which darkness and light are both alike. As this decay of the glacier takes place, and it is always more rapid near the lower border of it than above, the pressure of the upper masses brings the whole mountain slowly along: with a steadiness of march that cannot be perceived by the eye, but which is marked with precision, and chronicled from year to year. The place where great rocks are reposing on the surface near the edge of the mountain against which the glacier presses has been carefully noted, and the next year and for many subsequent years, the onward progress of the boulder has been noted. Blocks of granite have been inserted in the bosom of the glacier, and their position defined by their relation to the points of land in sight; and years afterwards they are away on their journey, and by and by, they have disappeared altogether as the glacier moves on and heaves and breaks and closes again. More wonderful still, it is recorded that a "mass of granite of twenty six thousand cubic feet, originally buried under the snow, was raised to the surface and even elevated above it upon two pillars of ice, so that a small army might have found shelter under it." The men of science who have pursued investigations here under circumstances quite as fearful and forbidding as the navigators around the north Pole, have a rude hut in which they make themselves as comfortable as the nature of the case will admit; but this house though founded on a rock is not stationary. It moves on with the mighty field of ice, about three hundred feet in a year, or nearly one foot every day: not so rapidly in winter as in summer, for the rate of progress depends on the melting, which is arrested for a brief period during the terrible winters of this Alpine region. Other glaciers move with greater rapidity than this. The Mere de Glace is believed to move at the rate of four or five hundred feet every year, and it is said that the glacier is gradually wasting out.

The surface of this frozen sea is exceedingly irregular, depending on the nature of the ground below, and the progress of the ice. When a stream has cut away a great seam, where the descent of the moving mass will be swift when it does move, the shock will throw up the ice in ridges, in pyramids, in various fantastic shapes, piling rocks on rocks of ice, as if some great explosion underneath had upheaved the surface and the fragments had come down in wild confusion, like the ruins of a crystal city. Then the sun gradually melts those towers, and they assume strange shapes of wild and dazzling beauty, unreal palaces, glittering minarets, silvered domes and shining battlements; freaks of nature we call them, but they are too beautiful for chance work, and we do not know to what eyes these forms of glory may give pleasure, nor why it is that God displays so much of his selectest skill and most stupendous power, where few behold it of the race to which we belong. Doubtless our own great Cataract leaped and thundered in the wilderness thousands of years, with no human ear or eye to receive its majesty and beauty, but it did not roar in vain. God has other and nobler worshippers than man, and while we are groping like moles beneath the surface, and striving in our blindness to discover the mysteries of God's works, there are minds to which these wonders are revelations of their Maker's glory and goodness, and they understand, admire and adore.

Here was a world of solid water, gradually enlarging and then melting away, to send down rivers into the plains below, and this with the other glaciers of the Alps, is thus supplying all the rivers in Europe which might otherwise be dry. Yet as other rivers in other lands are constantly supplied without this provision, we must suppose that some other design in Providence is laid, which science may or may not discover, but whether it does or not, we are certain that they are not without a purpose corresponding with the magnitude of their proportions, and the wisdom of Him who, though omnipotent, never wastes His strength in works without design.

We confined our walks to the edges of this solid but still treacherous sea. We had yesterday conversed with a man who had fallen into the crevices of one of these glaciers, and we had a greater horror of repeating the experiment. The case is on record of a shepherd who was crossing this very glacier with his flock, when he fell into one of the clefts, into which a torrent was pouring. This stream was his guide to life and liberty again; for he followed its course under the archway it had made, until it led him to the foot of the glacier into the open air. But a Swiss clergyman, a spiritual shepherd, M. Mouron, was leaning on the edge of a fissure to explore a remarkable formation over the brink, when the staff on which he rested gave way, and he fell, only to be drawn out again a mangled corpse. A man was let down by a rope, and after two or three unsuccessful expeditions, found him at last, and was drawn up with the body in his arms.

Coming down from the hill, we had hard work in crossing some dangerous clefts in the rocks, and once

I planted my Alpen-stock firmly, as I thought, in the
thin soil, and leaped; the spike failed; the foot of
the staff slipped on and left the steel in the ground,
and I was sprawling generally along down the hill:
fortunately I recovered my foothold, and came down
standing! And this is a good place in which to say
that shoes with iron nails in the soles are not the best
for walking over these mountains: a good pair of
boots with double soles have served me many times,
sticking fast in the face of a slippery rock, while
travellers shod with iron have been sliding down
with no strength of sole to resist the gravitation.
But I met with no such misfortune in all my travels
over the most dangerous passes, and under circumstances of trial not often exceeded by those who
wander in these parts.

We had several sorts of weather in this expedition
to the source of the Aar. The misty morning was
succeeded by a glowing sun at noon, followed by
clouds and rain. When this was coming, we thought
it time to be going, and gathering a few flowers,
as usual, on the verge of the cold beds of ice, we
turned our weary steps towards the Hospice. It
was our good fortune just then to meet an Italian
artist who had lost his way, and we had the pleasure
of guiding him to the Hospice. Wandering with his
knapsack and port folio, in search of the beautiful

in nature, which he sketched by the way, it was of no great consequence to him, in which direction he travelled, but a storm was now at hand, it was rapidly growing cold, and he was going every moment farther from any place of shelter.

We were soon housed safely in the Hospice; and glad enough to stretch ourselves on a bed after the walk of the morning. It was hard to keep warm anywhere else but in bed. The house was yet so unfinished and open, and the storm increasing every moment; a wretched old stove in one corner of the eating-roon, scarcely giving any heat with the few sticks of fuel we were able to find. We wrapped blankets around us, and tried to write, and when that proved to be more than we could accomplish under the difficulties, I took my Bible and read to my German friend some of the sublimest passages in the Psalms, where the Lord is revealed among the mountains, and his majesty portrayed by the loftiest of his works. He listened with interest, and when I laid aside the book, he asked for it, and read it long and earnestly.

As the evening drew on, a few travellers began to drop in, and at seven o'clock a company, much like the one of last night, but all with new faces, sat down to supper.

CHAPTER VII.

MOUNTAINS, STREAMS AND FALLS.

Pedestrianism—Mountain Torrents—Fall of the Handek—The Guide and his Little Ones—Falls of the Reichenbach—Perilous Point of View.

OT in the best of spirits, nor in as good condition as a pedestrian could wish, I set off the next morning, with my young friends. We would have felt better but for a foolish resolution to carry our own knap-sacks and overcoats and to make one day's journey without guide or mule. Success is apt to make one proud; and we had improved so much in our walking with each day's experience, that we actually began to think we could do anything in that line. The storm of the night before had gone by, and a clear cool day encouraged us. Alas, we knew not

(122)

how soon, in the midst of glaciers, and in sight of dazzling snow-drifts, the hot sun would thaw our resolution, and compel us to call lustily for help, when no Hercules would be at hand to lend us aid.

Not a wilder or more romantic path had we found than the one which led us out of the vale of the Grimsel. The river Aar is by our side, leaping from ledge to ledge in its rapid descent; dashing now against rocks and foaming around them and onward, as if maddened by every obstacle and brooking no delay. Water in motion is always beautiful. Here on our right hand a streamlet is falling from the giddy height of a thousand feet above us. At first it slips along on the edge of the rocks, as if afraid to fall, and then with a graceful bound it clears the side of the mountain, and comes down to a lower level, where it reposes for a moment in a basin made without hands, and again it flows along down like a long white robe suspended on the hill side, tastefully winding itself, as in folds.

In full view, but far above us the snow lies fresh and white, for much of it fell there yesterday: and among the clouds as they roll open and let us see their beds, the blue glacier lies. Some of the views along here are exceedingly grand, and in the midst of barrenness that can hardly be excelled, the soul feels that enough is here to make a world, though there is little vegetation, and not a human habitation. We frequently cross the torrent by narrow bridges, and pause on each of them to watch the angry waters whirling underneath. I was arrested on one of them by the sight of a reservoir hollowed out of the solid rock by the water; it would hold twenty barrels, and was full. The torrent was now raving a few inches below, while the water within was as placid in the sunshine as if it had never moved. The contrast was beautiful. Let the mad world rush by, noisy, turbulent and thoughtless: it is better to be calm and trusting: certainly it is better if our rest is on a rock which cannot be moved.

The mountains rise suddenly from the edge of the torrent, and there is barely room in some places for the path and the stream. There is great danger too in travelling here in the winter when the avalanches come rushing down the precipitous sides of these mountains. Their work of destruction is lying all around us. They sweep across the path and for a long distance have laid the rock perfectly bare, and polished it so smoothly, that there is constant danger of sliding off into the gulf by the side of the way. Grooves have been cut in the rock, that the feet of the mules may have some support, but a prudent traveller will trust to his own feet and his staff, and tread cautiously. We become so accustomed to

these dangerous places, that we pass them without
emotion ; but there is never a season without its fatal
accidents to travellers, and none but fool-hardy persons will needlessly expose their lives.   An American
family returned home a few days ago, having left the
mangled corpse of their son, a lad of twelve years, in
some frightful gorge into which he had fallen while
riding on a mule in the midst of the Alps.   We frequently hear of painful facts like these, yet there is
not a pass in Switzerland which may not be safely
made with prudence and coolness.

One of the finest cascades we had yet seen was on
our right, after we had made about five miles from
the hospice.   Its width of stream, volume of water,
and great height, entitle it to a name and a record
which it has not ; and this has frequently appeared to
me strange in this journey ; that *falls* in Switzerland,
of comparatively little beauty, have been painted and
praised the world over, while others of more romantic
and impressive features have no place in the hand-
books, but are strictly anonymous.   The one we are
now speaking of, attracted our attention as decidedly
more interesting than any we had seen among the
mountains, and in this opinion I presume others will
agree.   Its misfortune is that it is within a mile of
the HANDEK, which we are now approaching.   A
huge log-hut received us, and we found refreshments

such as **might** be expected in a wilderness **like this.**
Sour **bread** and **sour** wine, with strong **cheese, and a**
strange-looking pie, composed of materials into which
it **was not** prudent to inquire, gave us a lunch **that**
might have been worse. We were glad to get it, **but**
even **more pleased** to find a **place** where we could lay
down our **burdens, under which** we had been groaning
for an hour. This pedestrianism in the Alps is very
well to **talk about, but** it is **not the most** agreeable
mode of travelling to one who is accustomed only to
a sedentary life. We could find no mules here, however, **but** meeting a sturdy **fellow who was going up**
the pass, and who was a guide **but** not **just now**
engaged, we made a bargain with him to turn about
and carry our **traps to** Meyringen. He was on his
way over the **Grimsel** into Canton Vallais to buy
eggs and butter, which he and his **son,** who was with
him, **would bring** back **to sell** in the lower valleys.
This is the **way** in which the traffic among the cantons is **chiefly** carried on. We are constantly meeting
the **traders, men** and women, with long baskets **or**
wooden cans on their backs, trudging over these
mountains, exchanging the produce of one part of the
country for **that** of another. **And** this business is
driven in winter as **well as** summer, and many lose
their lives in **the** snow, or are overwhelmed by the
avalanches. Our man now sent his boy on alone;

gave him a few directions as to what articles he should buy, and where to wait his return, and then set off with us. I was astonished that a father would trust a lad of such tender years (he was not more than twelve), to go off on such an expedition alone, in such a region as this; and after they had parted, I slipped some money into the little fellow's hand, and said a cheering word or two, for I felt as if it were cruel thus to leave him.

The river Aar has been rushing along by us, and now it has reached the verge of a precipice more than a hundred feet high. At this point another stream of only less volume forces its way across the path, and dashes boldly into the Aar on the brink of the fall. Like two frantic lovers they take the mad leap together into the fearful gulf. Standing above the brow of the fall, and looking into the dark abyss, where the vast column of water stands, silvered at the summit, spread and broken into foam as it reaches the base, with clouds of spray rising from the boiling depths below, we see a cataract that combines more of the sublime with the very beautiful than any other in Switzerland. After we had gazed upon it from the bridge at the brow, we went around and down through the forest, and reached the ledge from which we could look up and out upon the column of waters now pouring before us in exceeding strength. A faint rainbow trembled midway, but the pine trees were too thick to admit the sun's rays in full blaze upon the face of the fall. But the surrounding scenery adds so much to the gloomy grandeur of the scene, that I am quite willing to write this down as a *real* cataract, a wonderful leap and rush of waters, in the midst of a ravine of terrific construction; filling the mind with the strongest sense of wildness, horror, desolation and destruction, while the image of beauty in the water and the bow, plays constantly over the face of all. We left it with strong emotions of pleasurable excitement, and shall retain the recollections of the falls of the Aar for many days.

The path by and by led under an extraordinary projection of rock, shelving over, and making a pavilion. The descent became more rapid, until we took to a long flight of stone steps in the path : and then on a lower grade, we came upon meadow land, through which the grass had been cut away for foot passengers to make a shorter course than that by which the horses must find their way down. We entered a little cottage and refreshed ourselves *again*, with coffee and milk, and had some pleasant talk with the old lady and one or two of the neighbors who had dropped down from some mountain home ; for it is even pleasant, if no useful knowledge is gathered, to learn the thoughts and feelings of these secluded

people, and to find that enjoyment, and contentment
can exist as truly and beautifully in the dreary
heights of these Alpine pasturages, as in the courts
of kings : and a little more so.

For we were not very far above a lovely valley,
one of the sweetest spots that I carry in my memory.
It is surprising how suddenly the line of barrenness
is passed, and the region of fruits and abundant
vegetation bursts upon you in this country. We had
not been two hours from dreary and inhospitable
Guttanen, when we emerged from the narrow defile
into a vale, a plain, a basin of rare loveliness for
situation and embellishment. Level as a threshing
floor, with a hundred Swiss cotages scattered over it,
and each of them surrounded with a garden stored
with fruits, apples, pears, and the like, while a stream
flowing through the midst of it divided the vale into
two settlements, in one of which a neat church sent
up its graceful spire. We had been loitering along
down, and it was now drawing toward evening : the
bell of the old church was ringing for evening
prayers, and the people, a few of them, were gathering in their sanctuary as we passed. Four mountains, each of them a distinct pyramid, rise on as
many sides of this valley, and seem at once to shut
it from the world, and to stand around it as towers
of defence, as the mountains are round about

Jerusalem. This is the Vale of Upper Hasli; the river Aar flows through it; on the right as we are going, is the village of Im-Hof, and on the left the settlement is called Im-Grund. We passed a low house, like all the rest, and three little children in a row, broke out with a song, a sweet Psalm tune, such as our Sabbath school children would sing. We stopped to listen, and the guide stood with us in front of the group, while they sang one after another of their native melodies as birds of the forest would warble an evening song. The youngest was not more than two years old; and when we had given them some money for their music, I took the little thing by the hand, and said, " Come away with me." The guide took it by the other, and it trotted along between us with so much readiness, that it occurred to me instantly that these might be the children of the man who was with me. I said to him, " Are these yours?" " Yes Sir," said he, and catching up the little thing in his arms, he kissed it fondly, and carried it on with all the burdens already on his back. When he had put it down and the children had returned, I asked him why it was that no sign of recognition passed between him and his children when we first came up to them as they stood by the side of the house. He told me that he had taught them to receive him in this way when he came by with strangers, whom he was guiding, and as they sang to receive what money might be given them it was better that it should not be known there was any relation between him and them. I had detected the connection by the willingness of the babe to follow us, and the father was delighted to be able to discover himself to his child, and to take it for a moment in his arms. This incident reminded me of a striking scene in the well known history of William Tell, where the tyrant Gessler confronts the son with the father, and they both, without preconcert, but by a common instinct of caution, deny one another, and persist in the denial till the father is about to die.

Leaving the valley, we have a sharp hill to climb. A zig-zag path for carriages has been made over it at great expense of money and labor; so that this vale may be reached from the other side. The hill must at some distant period in the past have resisted the progress of the Aar, and this romantic valley was probably a beautiful lake in the midst of these noble mountains. But the hill by some convulsion has been rent from the top to the bottom, and the river finds its way through a fearful cavern; one of the most awful gorges that can be found in Switzerland. After crossing the hill we left the road, and following our guide for twenty minutes came to

the mouth of the cave, that leads down to the bed of
the river, where it is rushing through with frightful
force in darkness but not silence ; for the roar of
the waters is repeated among the rocks, adding
greatly to the terror of the scene. It is only half an
hour's walk from the Cave to Meyringen ; but we
made it more than an hour, enjoying the fine views
that opened upon us as we stood above the village.
It is but three miles across the plain, and as I look
upon the splendid cataract of the Reichenback falling into it on one side, and the Alpback coming
down on the other, and streaming cascades in great
numbers pouring into it down the precipitous sides
of the mountains, the first thought that strikes the
mind is of the danger that the valley would be filled
with water one of these days and the people driven
out. Such a calamity has indeed occurred, and to
guard against its return, a stone dyke one thousand
feet long and eight feet wide has been built, that the
swollen river may be conducted with safety out of
the vale. Long years ago the mountain torrent
brought down a mass of earth with it, so suddenly
and so fearfully that in one brief hour, a large part
of the village was buried twenty feet deep, and the
desolation thus wrought still appears over the whole
face of the plain. The Church has a black line
painted on it to mark the height to which it was

filled with the mud and water in this deluge of 1762. There is something very fearful in the idea of dwelling in a region subject to such visitations. But there is a fine race of men and women here. The men are spoken of as models for strength and agility, and the matches and games in which they annually contend with the champions of other cantons decide their claims to the distinction. The women are good looking, and that is more than I can say for most of the women I have met among the Alps; where the hardy, exposed, and toilsome life they lead, in poverty and disease, gives them such a look as I cannot bear to see in a female face. In fact I could not tell a man from a woman but by their dress in many parts of the mountains. Now we are down in the region of improved civilization, and some taste in dress begins to appear among the women, who rig themselves out in a holiday or Sunday suit of black velvet bodice, white muslin sleeves, a yellow petticoat, and a black hat set jauntingly on one side of the head, with their braided hair hanging down their backs. An old woman on the hill at whose house I stopped for a drink, told me I ought to stay there till next Sunday and see them all come out of church; "a prettier sight I would never see in all my life."

Coming down from the Hospice of the Grimsel, I was filled with admiration when I entered the valley in which the villages of Im-Hof and Im-Grund lie, with their single church and hundred cottages. Naigle, my guide, was one of the dwellers in this vale, and the meeting with his children as he passed through had deeply interested me in the place and the people. I wished to know more of their habits and especially I would know the spirit and the power of the religion which these people professed. They are so secluded from all the world, so girt with great mountains and compelled to look upwards whenever they would see far, that it seemed to me they must be a thoughtful religious people, even if their way of religion was not the same as mine. It was a Protestant Canton, and so far their faith was mine, but there is a wide difference between the faith and practice of many churches that profess Protestantism, as there is also in the churches under the dominion of the Pope of Rome.

Naigle was a character. I was sure of it in five minutes after he was in my service. Six feet high on a perpendicular, he was at least six feet four, on a curve, for long service in carrying heavy burdens over the mountains had made a bend in his back like a bow that is never unstrung. I had asked him how many of those children he had, and he had told me eight: and he did not improve in my good opinion when he offered as the only objection to selling

me the youngest, that he would be sent to prison if
he did.   Yet Naigle loved his children I am sure,
and would not part with one of them unless for the
sake of improving its prospects for the future.   His
own were dark enough.   One franc a day, less than
twenty cents of our money, is the price of a day's
labor in the hardest work of the year, though the
very men who are glad to get this of their neighbors,
will not guide a stranger through their country, or
carry his bag, for less than five francs for eight or ten
hours.   The women will work out doors all day for
less than a man's wages, and perform the same kind
of labor.   This Naigle was a hard-working man, it
was very plain, and there was a decided streak of
good sense in him that assured me, he could give me
much valuable information, in spite of that miserable mixture of German and French which was the
only language he could speak.   Fortunately I
had my young German friend with me, and we managed among us to extract from Naigle all we desired.
We had good rooms at Meyringen, and Naigle was
to stay over night there and return to his family in
the morning.   I asked him where he would sleep;
and he said "in the stable," a lodgment I afterwards
found to be common in this and other European countries: not in rooms fitted up over the stalls, as in
America, but in bunks by the side of the horses: in

the midst of foul atmosphere which would be enough,
I should suppose, to stifle any man in the course of
the night. Yet I have heard a German gentleman
say that there is no smell so pleasant to him as that
of a stable, and I record it as another evidence of the
truth of the adage " there is no disputing about *tastes*."
Naigle came up to my room in the evening, sat
down on a trunk, and answered questions for an hour
or two, but I can put all I learned of him into a moderate compass, though it will want the freshness and
often the peculiar turn of thought with which he
imparted it.

Naigle told me first of his family which he had
great difficulty in supporting on the low wages he
received, and the small profits he could make on his
trade with the neighboring valleys. At least half of
the year, he said, they do not have a particle of meat
in the house : they live chiefly on potatoes and beans,
with bread and milk : few vegetables, and these not
the most nutritious. The snow comes on so early in
autumn and lies so late in the spring that the season
for cultivation is very short, though they try to make
the most of it while it lasts, as they do of the little
land in their valley, and on the mountain sides. Yet
poverty often stares them in the face with a melancholy threat of famine. No people on earth dwell in

such glorious scenery and in such destitution of the real comforts of life.

But what are the morals of such a people? Are the virtues of social life held in honor among them, and are the children of these mountain homes trained up in the way they should go? One of the severest replies I have had was given to me by a Swiss guide, who had followed his business of showing strangers through the country for thirty years: and when he told me he had three sons grown up to manhood I asked him if they were guides also? He said, " No, he never allowed them to travel about with foreigners: the boys learned too many bad words and ways in that business." Very likely intercourse with travellers is not happy on the morals of any people, but it is little that the dwellers in these valleys see of foreigners, who push through them without pausing even to spend a night. Naigle gave me however to understand that the standard of social morals was very low among them, and this was confirmed by all that I learned from the various classes of men with whom I came in contact during my journey in this country. It is true everywhere, that virtue does not flourish in the extremes of poverty or wealth.

He was greatly interested in the little church, and was pleased to answer all my inquiries. The pastor, he said, was a good man who was kind to them in

sickness, visiting them to give the consolations of the
gospel, and especially at such times did they prize his
instructions and prayers.   This service was rendered
freely to the poorest among them, on whom the pastor
calls as soon as he hears that they are in distress, and
he is always engaged in looking among his flock to
find those who have need of his peculiar care.   The
same good shepherd has charge of the parish school,
to which all the children are sent ; and if the parents
are able to pay anything toward their children's education, they are expected to do so, but if not they are
not deprived of the privileges of the school.   Here
they are taught to read, to write, and to keep accounts ; but more than all this, they are instructed in
the catechism of the church, and are examined often
on it, and encouraged to become acquainted with the
doctrines and duties of religion.   It was hard for me to
convey my idea to Naigle when I sought to learn of
him, if the good pastor required of the young people
any proof of *regeneration*, or a change of heart, before
giving them the second sacrament.   He said their
children are all baptized in infancy, and admitted to
the Lord's Supper when they are old enough, and
good enough, and understand the doctrines taught in
the school.

   " But what if one of those who has come to the

holy sacrament falls into some sin, as stealing, or pro-
fane swearing?"

"O, in that case he is not allowed to come to the
sacrament, till he has repented and reformed. The
minister is very strict about that, and the people who
belong to the church, that is, those who wish to be
considered as good Christian people, never indulge in
any of those things which are forbidden by the Bible.
There are many loose people in the valley who have
no care for God or man, but have no connection with
the church."

On the whole, I was led to infer from what Naigle
said that the church of the Upper Hasli valley is
about in the same condition with hundreds of others
in this and other lands. There is in the midst of this
mountain scenery far removed from the intercourse
of the world, where a newspaper is rarely seen, and
few books are ever read, a little people among whom
God has some friends, who in their way are striving
to serve him, and whose service it will be pleasure to
accept. Many of them have only a form of religion.
The Romish religion that surrounds these lands, and
which is so admirably framed for an ignorant and
sensual people, pervades the minds of many who are
Protestants in name, and who cannot be taught, or
rather will not learn, that salvation is only by faith
in the Saviour. That other gospel which gives heav-

en to him who does penance for his great sins, and
bows often to the picture of a handsome woman, is
the religion for a people who cannot read, or who
have no books if they can. Ignorance and Romanism
go hand in hand.

My estimate of the Swiss character has wofully de-
preciated since I have travelled among these mountains. With a history such as Greece might be proud
of, and a race of heroes that Rome never excelled in
the days when women would be mothers only to have
sons for warriors ; the Swiss people now are at a point
of national and social depression painful to contemplate. They are indebted largely to the defences of
nature for the comparative liberty they enjoy, and
perhaps to the same seclusion is to be referred their
want of a thousand comforts of life, which an improved state of society brings. All the romance of a
Swiss cottage is taken out of a traveller's mind, the
moment he enters one of these cabins and seeks refreshment or rest. The saddest marks of poverty meet
him in the door. The same roof is the shelter of the
man, woman and beast. The same room is often the
bed chamber of all. Scanty food, and that miserably
prepared, is consumed without regard to those domestic arrangements which make life at home a luxury.
There is no *future* to the mind of a Swiss youth. He
lives to live as his father lived—and that is the end

of life with him. Perhaps he may have a gun, and in that case, to be the best shot in the valley may fill his ambition : or if he is strong in the arms and legs he may aim at distinction in the games which once a year are held at some hamlet in the Canton, where the wrestlers and runners contend for victory, and others throw weights and leap bars as of old in Greece, when kings were not ashamed to enter the lists. Many of the youth of Switzerland are willing to sell themselves into the service of foreign powers, as soldiers—Swiss soldiers—hired to be shot at, and shoot any body a foreign despot may send them to slay : a service so degrading, and at the same time so decidedly hazardous to life and limb, with so poor a chance for pay, that none but a people far gone in social degradation would be willing thus to make merchandise of their blood. Yet they have fought battles bravely with none of the stimulus of patriotism, and their blood has been as freely poured out for tyrants who hired them, as if they were bleeding for their own and the land of William Tell.

Falls of the Reichenbach.

I had enjoyed all the pleasures of pedestrianism that I wished, and told Naigle to get me a horse for to-morrow. He was willing to go on with us for a day or two more, but I gave him a trifle for his wife, and to pay him for his evening while I kept him talking when he would have **been** sleeping; and after he had brought me a man who would go with his horse, and carry me on over the Wengern Alp, I dismissed him. There is nothing in Swiss travelling more annoying than the impositions practised upon you by those who have horses or mules for hire. The price for a horse is at the rate usually of about ten francs or two dollars a **day**; but if you are not to return the **next day to the place from which** you started, (and **you rarely or** never do,) you must pay the same price for the horse to come back. The driver manages **to** find a traveller to come back with, and so gets double pay both ways in nine trips out of ten. If the business were left open to competition without the help of government, the price would be reduced. Naigle brought me **a man who would go** with his horse as **far as** I liked for **ten francs a day, and** nothing for return money, but he desired me to set off in the morning **on** foot, and he would be **a** few minutes off, **out of the** village, for if the landlords who keep horses to let, knew that he was at the business on his own hook, **they** would molest him. **He served** me well, and I paid **him to his entire** satisfaction.

Leaving Meyringen **on a** lovely morning, the last of August, crossing the **Aar by a** bridge, I came at once **to the Baths of Reichenbach,** where there is a

good hotel, said to be better than those at Meyringen. The grounds about are tastefully arranged, and
an establishment fitted up for invalids, with every
convenience for warm and cold baths on a moderate
scale. If plenty of mountain water and mountain air
will make sick people well, here is a fine place for
them to come and be cured. I climbed the mountain in haste, to get the finer view of the Reichenbach Fall, whose roar I had heard, and the spray of
which was rising continually before me. I could see
the torrent as it took its first leap out of the forest,
but it plunged instantly out of sight into a deep
abyss, and I must ascend to its brow, and see the
rush of waters as they descend into the gorge. The
path to those coming down is very difficult, so steep,
indeed, that it is safer and pleasanter to leave the
horse and come on foot. But we went up slowly till
we reached a meadow of table land, which we were
permitted to cross on paying a small toll, to a house
which has been built at the point where the best
view of the fall from below can be had. It is almost
a shame to board up such scenes as these, and compel
a man to look through a window at a scene where he
would have nothing around him but the mountain,
flood and sky. The young woman was very civil,
and offered us woodwork for sale, and a view through
colored glass, and a subscription-book to record our

donations for the construction of the foot-path, and we finally had the privilege of taking a look in silence. A narrow, but no mean **stream**, plunging TWO THOUSAND feet makes a cataract before which the spectator stands with awe. The leap is not made at once, yet the river rests but twice in all that distance, and only for a moment then. The point of view where we are now beholding it, is midway of the upper and grandest of these successive falls. The fury of the descending torrent is terrible. The spray rises in perpetual clouds from the dread abyss into which the river leaps. It might be a bottomless **abyss**, so far as human penetration can discover, for no arm can fathom it, no eye can pierce the dark cavern where the waters boil and roar, and whence they issue only to make another leap into the vale below. The bow of God is on the brow of the cataract. I do so love to find it there, not more for its exceeding beauty than the feeling of hope and safety it always inspires. We counted all the colors as it waved and smiled so fondly in the spray, as if it loved its birth-place.— Having had the finest opportunity of seeing the fall from this point, we did not return across the field to the horses, but took the foot-path straight up the mountain, over a rough and toilsome way, led on by a little lad who seemed anxious to do us the favor. He guided us by a walk of twenty minutes to the brink of the precipice. The path was just wide enough for one person to pass around the headland, holding by the bushes as we walked, and thus by taking turns in the perilous excursion, we went to the brow of the cataract, and looked down the front of the terrific fall. A single misstep or the slipping of a foot, might plunge the curious gazer into the gulph; yet so seductive and so flattering is such danger, we rarely have the least sense of it till it is over. Not the water only, but the whole prospect from this overhanging cliff, is in a high degree sublime. The plains of Meyringen, the mountains beyond, from which cascades are hanging like white lace vails on the green hill-sides, villages and scattered cottages, the river Aar shooting swiftly across the valley, are now in full view, and we turn away reluctantly from the sight to resume the ascent.

7

CHAPTER VIII

A GLACIER AND AVALANCHE.

Alpine Horn—Beggars—The Rosenlaui Glacier—Beautiful Views—Glorious Mountain Scenes—Mrs. Kinney's "Alps"—A Lady and Babe—The Great Scheidek—Grindelwald—Eagle and Bear—Battle with Bugs—Wengern Alp—A real Avalanche—The Jungfrau.

 BEAUTIFUL Chamois was standing on the ledge of rock that overhung the path as I turned away from the Reichenbach Fall, and I was pleased to see so fine a specimen of the animal whose home is the Alps and whose pursuit has for ages been the delight of the mountaineer. He would have sprung from crag to crag at my approach and soon disappeared, had he not been held by a string in the hand of a boy who expected a few coppers for showing the animal. This is but one of a hundred ways and

(146)

means of begging adopted by the Swiss peasantry. Of all ages from the infant to extreme decrepitude, they plant themselves along the highways of travel, and by every possible pretext seek to obtain the pence of the traveller. Some are glad to have a poor cretin or a case of goitre in the family, that they may have an additional plea to put in for charity. Others sing or play on some wretched instrument, and the traveller would cheerfully pay them something to be silent, that he may enjoy the beauties of the world around him without the torment of their music. But the Alpine Horn makes music to which the hills listen. A wooden tube nearly ten feet long and three inches in diameter, curved at the mouth which is slightly enlarged, is blown with great strength of lungs, and the blast at first harsh and startling is caught by the mountain sides and returned in softened strains, echoing again and again as if the spirits of the wood were answering to the calls of the dwellers in the vales. The man who was blowing, had but one hand, and after a single performance, or one blast, he held out that hand for his pay, and then returned to his instrument, making the hills to resound again with his wild notes.

The Rosenlaui valley into which we now enter is a green and sunny plain, where the verdure is as rich and the fruits as fair as if there were no oceans of

never melting ice and hills of snow lying all around
and above it.   On either side the bare mountains rise
perpendicularly : the Engel-Horner or Angel's Peaks
sending their shining summits so far into the heavens
that the pagans would make them the thrones of
gods, and the Well-Horn, and Wetter-Horn, bleak
and cold, but now replendent in a brilliant sun light.
A small but very comfortable inn is fitted up in this
valley with conveniences for bathing, and a few invalids are always here for the benefit of the air, scenery
and the mountain baths.   We rested at the tavern,
and then walked a mile out of the way to see the Glacier of the Rosenlaui.   After a short ascent we
entered a fine forest, and followed the gorge through
which the glacier torrent is rushing : an awful gorge
a thousand feet deep it seemed to me, and if some
mighty shock has not rent these rocks, and opened
the way for the waters that are now roaring in
those dark mysterious depths, they must have been
a thousand years in wearing out the channel for
themselves.   A slight bridge is thrown across the
ravine, and a terrible pleasure there is in standing
on it and listening to the mad leaps of rocks which
the peasants are prepared to launch into the abyss,
for the amusement of travellers.   I shuddered at
the thought of falling, and felt a glow of pleasing
relief when I was away from the tempting verge.   I

never could explain to myself the source of that half formed desire which so many, perhaps all have, of trying the leap when standing on the brow of a cataract, the verge of a precipice, the summit of a lofty tower. It is often a question whether persons who have thus perished, designed to commit suicide or not. It is not unlikely that some are suddenly seized with this undefined desire to make the trial: the mind is wrought into a frenzy of excitement, dizziness ensues, and in a moment of fear, desire and delirium the irresponsible victim leaps into the gulf. Many of the fearful passes of the Alps have their local tragedies of this sort, and I was not disposed to add another. We soon climbed to the foot of the glacier. We have come to a mountain of emerald. The sun is shining on it, at high noon. The melting waters have cut a glorious gateway of solid crystal: we step within and beneath the arch. A ledge of ice affords a standing place for the cool traveller who may plant his pike staff firmly and look over into the depths where the torrent has wrought its passage and from which the mists are curling upwards. The sunlight streams through the blue domes of these caverns, long icicles sparkle in the roof, and jewels, crowns and thrones of ice are all about me in this crystal cave. Its outer surface is remarkable for the purity of the ice, its perfect freedom from that deposit of earth and broken stone which mars the beauty of most of the glaciers of Switzerland. Great white wreaths are twisted on its brow, and on its bosom palaces and towers are brilliant in the sunlight; and from the side of it the Well-horn and Wetter-horn rise like giants from their bed, and stretch themselves away into the clouds. No sight among the Alps had so charmed me with its beauty and sublimity. These hills of pure ice, this great gateway only less bright in the sun than the gates of pearl, cold indeed, but with flowers and evergreens cheating the senses into the feeling that this is not real, it must be a reproduction of fabled palaces and hills of diamonds, and mountains of light. I am sure that I do not exaggerate: the memory of it now that I recur to it after many days is of great glory, such as the eye never can see out of Switzerland, and the forms of beauty and the thoughts of majesty, awakened as I stood before and beneath and upon this glacier, must remain among the latest images that will fade from the soul.

Excited by what I had seen and mindless of the path by which I had ascended, I threw myself back upon my Alpen-stock and slid down the face of a long shelving rock, leaping when I could, and gliding when the way was smooth, and reached the bridge and the ravine in safety, though the guides insisted that the longest way around was the surest way down. We are now at the foot of lofty mountains. The warm sun is loosening the masses of snow and ice and we are constantly hearing the roar of the avalanches. At first it startles us, as if behind the clear blue sky above us there is a gathering storm: the sound comes rushing down and multiplied by echoes themselves re-echoed from the surrounding hills, the thunder is forgotten in the majesty of this music of the mountains. We see nothing from which these voices came. There are valleys beyond these peaks where perhaps the foot of man has never trod, and He who directs the thunderbolt when it falls, is guiding these ice-falls into the depths of some abyss where they may not crush even one of the least of the creatures of his care. It is grand to hear them and feel that they will not come nigh us. Our path is now so far from the base of this precipitous mountain that if those snow caps fall, and we are constantly wishing that they would, we should be in no peril, and so we ride on with hearts full of worship, rejoicing in the thoughts of Him who built these high places, and whose praise is uttered in the silence of all these speechless peaks, and shouted in the avalanche in tones which seem to be reverberated all around the world. One of our own poets, with a soul in harmony with the greatness

as well as the beauty of this scenery, exclaims in view
of these towering heights—

> Eternal pyramids, built not with hands,
>   From linked foundations that deep-hidden lie,
> Ye rise apart, and each a wonder stands !
>   Your marble peaks, that pierce the clouds so high,
>   Seem holding up the curtain of the sky
> And there, sublime and solemn, have ye stood
>   While crumbling Time, o'erawed, passed reverent by—
> Since Nature's resurrection from the flood,
> Since earth, new-born, again received God's plaudit, " Good !"
>
> Vast as mysterious, beautiful as grand !
>   Forever looking into Heaven's clear face,
> Types of sublimest Faith, unmoved ye stand,
>   While tortured torrents rave along your base :
>   Silent yourselves, while, loosed from its high place,
> Headlong the avalanche loud thundering leaps !
>   Like a foul spirit, maddened by disgrace,
> That in its fall the souls of thousands sweeps
> Into perdition's gulf, down ruin's slippery steeps.
>
> Dread monuments of your Creator's power !
>   When Egypt's pyramids shall mouldering fall,
> In undiminished glory ye shall tower,
>   And still the reverent heart to worship call,
>   Yourselves a hymn of praise perpetual;
> And if at last, when rent is Law's great chain,
>   Ye with material things must perish all,
> Thoughts which ye have inspired, not born in vain,
> In immaterial minds for aye shall live again.

My mind was full of such thoughts as these, so
finely clothed in Mrs. Kinney's words, when I met a
party of ladies and gentlemen, and one of the ladies

was borne along in a chair, with a babe in her arms! Here was a contrast, and a suggestive sight. It was certainly the pursuit of knowledge under difficulties, but I could readily understand that having overcome every obstacle in her strong desire to see the Alps, and to see them now, she was enjoying them perhaps more than any one of the group around her. And I did not fail to admire the energy of soul that in its love of nature, and its thirsting after these mighty manifestations of power and beauty, was equal to all the difficulties that opposed her way. Whether ladies may make these difficult passes, which must be made to see the inner life and real character of Switzerland, is merely a question of dollars and cents. The feeblest may be borne as tenderly as this infant was on its mother's breast, and the most delicate will gather health and strength from the bracing mountain air, and new life will be inspired in the midst of these exciting scenes. To see Switzerland on wheels is impracticable. Its brightest glories are hid away in regions of perpetual ice and snow, where no traveller passes except to *see*. The highways of trade are not here. This is a secret place of the Most High, where from the foundation of the world, he has wrapt himself in storms and clouds, and thundered among the hills, and has been admired only by those who have come here expressly to behold his works. The solitude of such scenery adds intensely to the sense of the sublime. Mountains all around us and God! To be alone with him anywhere is to be near him: in the midnight, or on the ocean or the desert, it is a heart-luxury to feel that only God is near; that his presence fills immensity, and his Spirit pervades all matter and all space. But to stand in the midst of these great Alps, hoary patriarchs, monuments compared with which the pyramids are children of a day, is to stand in the high places of his dominions and to be raised by his own hand into audience with him at whose presence these mountains shall one day flow down like water and melt away. *Heinrich*, my young German friend, was peopling them continually with the creatures of Grecian mythology, and his classic history often led him to speak of the lofty seats of divinities where ancient poets had planted the council halls of the gods. I loved to believe that God had made these hills for himself, and as the people who dwell among them have no heart to appreciate them, pilgrims from all lands are flocking here, and offering the incense of praise at the foot of these high altars. How they do lead the soul along upward toward the great white throne! How like that throne is yonder peak in snowy purity shining now in this bright sun. It is very glorious, and no human foot-step ever trod the summit. God sits there alone.

Let us admire and adore. He is fearful in praises, doing wonders! Who is like unto him, a great God, and a great King!

But this is not getting on with the journey. You have the privilege of skipping my *reflections* as you read ; but to travel without reflection, common as it is, is not my way—and if you would feel the sights that meet the eye in this world of wonders, you must indulge me in pausing now and then, to muse. All this time we have been going steadily up the Great Scheidek, and have now stopped at a small house, with the word tavern painted on it in two or three different languages. An apology for a dinner we got after waiting for it till an appetite for supper came. The view from this height into the Grindelwald valley is enchanting. The descent is so steep that we were willing to leave the mules and walk down, holding back by the alpenstock, and resting often to enjoy the sight, into the valley below. And now we have come to another glacier, in the midst of a sunny slope, stretching down into the bosom of verdant pasturage where herds are grazing and flowers are blossoming, and women and children are laboring under a burning sun. It is hard to believe, even as we stand at the foot of it, that this is everlasting ice : a segment of the frozen zone let fall into the lap of summer, and sleeping here age after age, perishing con-

tinually, but renewed day by day, so that it seems
unchanged. It is a wonderful growth and decay ;
and the greater wonder to my mind, and one that
does not diminish, is that so much life and beauty can
exist and flourish in the midst of this eternal cold.——
Yet there is a greater contrast even here. We are
coming into the valley, and there another, called the
Upper Glacier lies, and yet that is not to furnish the
contrast of which I speak. It is in the wide and
wonderful difference between this people and their
country ! Degenerate, ignorant, begging and demor-
alized, this people seem, and indeed are, unworthy of
such a land as this. They have a history, but Switzerland was, and is not. The race has run down.——
Disease and hardships have reduced the stock, till
now we rarely meet a fine-looking man, never a fine-
looking woman, as we cross the mountains and trav-
erse the valleys of this noble country.

The vale of Grindenwald, into which we have now
descended, is one of the most fertile, picturesque, and
quiet in Switzerland. It is a place to stay in. The
hotels, of which there are two, are crowded to overflowing. We sent our guide ahead to get room for
for us, but he failed. There was no room for us at
the inn. We paused first at the *Eagle*, a very good-
looking establishment, and the balcony running across
the front of it was filled with good-looking people——

but there were as many there as the house would
hold, and we had to go on to the *Bear*. And the
Bear would not let us in. The very best the landlord
could do, was to give us a room with three beds in it,
in a *cottage* across the way, where we would be quiet
and comfortable. We went over. Up stairs, by as
dark, narrow, dirty, ricketty, dangerous and disagreeable a passage as I had made among the mountains,
we were led by a tall, skinny, slatternly woman, with
a tallow candle in her fingers, and shown into our
treble chamber. For the first time we were in such
a house as the better class of peasants occupy in
Switzerland. It had been taken by the proprietor of
the hotel, as a sort of makeshift when his hotel was
overflowing—the lower part of it was his bake and
wash house, and this room was reserved for lodgings.
I was worn out with the journey of the day, and glad
enough to stretch myself on any thing that ventured
to call itself a bed. The walls of the chamber around
and above were rude boards, and the bare floor had
been trodden a hundred years without feeling. The
furniture was a mixture of the broken chairs of the
hotel and the superannuated relics of the cottage, an
amusing study, which helped to pass away half an
hour, while our prison keeper, the ugly old woman,
was scaring up something for us to eat. Bread and
milk, with some cheese so strong that we begged her

to take it off, made a frugal repast, but sweet to a hungry man : this mountaineering does give a man an appetite— and then he sleeps so well after eating. Alas! my dreams were short ; a band of bloodthirsty villains attacked me in the dead of night, and for four hours I fought them tooth and nail. The battle made real the poet's description of another scene—

" Though hundreds, thousands bleed,
    Still **hundreds**, thousands, more succeed."

How many of the foe found that night a bed of death in my bed, I cannot say, as we took no account of the slain, but the conflict was sanguinary and the destruction of life was immense. The sun rose upon the battle field, but it was hard to say which was the victor. Exhausted quite as much by the night's exertions as the travels of the previous day, I rose to address myself to the journey. The rapacious landlord of the Bear charged us the same price for our lodgings that was paid by those who had the best rooms in his house, and I told him we were willing to pay him for the privilege of hunting in his grounds, which we had greatly enjoyed for several hours. He was too slow to take my meaning, but when he did, he had no idea there was any harm in a few fleas. All these mountain sides are covered with the huts of the shepherds, where during a part of the year a man remains to tend the flocks, and he takes with him some coarse food to last him during the months of his stay. The shepherds and their families live in the midst of their dogs and cattle, and fleas are no worse to them than they are to us. It only served to amuse the landlord of the *Bear*, when we related to him the sufferings of the night, and besought him never to expose travellers to such annoyances again.

The ascent of the *Faulhorn* is made from Grindelwald. It is a mountain eight thousand feet high, and the view from the summit is said to be an ample reward for the five hours' walk or ride which is necessary to gain it. The long and glorious range of the Bernese Alps stands majestically in sight, and there are not wanting those who declare the prospect superior to that which is had on the Rigi. I took it on trust, and having loftier summits still before me, was willing to leave the Faulhorn. And I was willing to leave Grindelwald too—glad to escape the scene of my midnight sufferings, but I doubt not that at the *Eagle* (and not at the Bear) we might have spent a day or two very pleasantly in this charming vale. And how soon are these little vexations of life forgotten. They are worth mentioning only to remind us how foolish it is to be vexed at trifles, which in a single day are with the things that happened a hundred years ago. Thus moralizing and

half sorry that I had made any complaint of my
quarters for the night, I mounted my horse and set
off to cross

The Wengern Alp.

The ride through the vale in the early morning
was refreshing. Parties of travellers were emerging
from cottages where they had found beds, and winding their way by the bridle paths, in various directions, on foot and on horseback, all seeking to see the
world of Switzerland, and all enjoying themselves
with the various degrees of ability which had been
given them. We crossed the lesser *Sheideck*, and
stopped on the ridge of it at a small house of
refreshment to eat Alpine strawberries and milk.
The berries are small and have very little of the
strawberry taste, but are quite a treat in their way.
They were apparently more abundant here than we
had seen them elsewhere, and with plenty of milk
they made a capital lunch. Well for us that we had
the milk before a dirty boy who was playing at the
door when we came up, plunged his mouth and nose
into the milkpan and took a long drink, only with-
drawing when his father wished to dip some out for a
lady who had just arrived. Had she seen the operation, she would have declined the draught, but where
" Ignorance is bliss 'tis folly to be wise."

We rested a few moments only at this chalet, and then pushed on, passing a forest, or the ruins of a forest, which the avalanches had mown down as grass. The stumps, and here and there a scraggy tree were the witnesses of the desolation that had been wrought. From the height we are crossing we have one of the most magnificent of Alpine views. The JUNGFRAU stands before us clad in white raiment, beautiful as a bride adorned for her husband : in the sunlight she is dazzling and seems so near to heaven, and so pure in her vestal robes, that we are willing to believe the gateway must be there. The name of this mountain Jungfrau, or the Virgin, is given, on account of the peculiar beauty and purity of the peak which until 1812 had never been sullied by the foot of man. Rising like a pyramid above the surrounding heights thirteen thousand seven hundred and forty-eight feet, and seeming to be as smooth as if cut with a chisel out of solid marble, she stands there sublimely beautiful, to be gazed at and admired. Lord Byron has made this region the scene of some of his most terrible passages, and I was forcibly impressed as I read them with the *contrast,* not the similarity, between his emotions and my own in the midst of these mountains. Here he conceived some of those images never read in his Manfred without a shudder. In his Journal he says

" the clouds rose from the opposite valley, curling up
perpendicular precipices like the foam of the ocean
of hell during a spring-tide—it was white and
sulphury, and immeasurably deep in appearance."
Then in Manfred he does it into verse:

> " The mists boil up around the glaciers : clouds
>   Rise curling fast beneath me white and sulphury,
>   Like foam from the roused ocean of deep hell
>   Whose every wave breaks on a living shore,
>   Heap'd with the damn'd like pebbles."

None but a mind surcharged with horrors, a mind
which all bad things inhabit, could find such images
to convey its emotions in view of these sights of
grandeur, beauty, and glory. The mists were curling along up the precipices as I have seen incense in
a great cathedral, mounting the lofty columns, and
curling among the arches, a symbol of the praise
that goes up from the hearts of worshippers to the
God of heaven. These white clouds, not " sulphury "
—so far from being suggestive of hell-waves, were
heavenly robes rather, and as the sun now nearly at
noon, was filling them with light, I loved to watch
them, and then look away up to the summit of the
mountains around me, rejoicing in the manifestations
which the King of kings was making of himself in
this dwelling among the munitions of rocks. With
those thoughts full on me as I rode along the verge

of the tremendous ravine that separates the Wengern Alp from the Jungfrau, we reached a small inn, on the brow of the ravine, where large parties, chiefly English people, were ravening for dinner. This house has been planted here in the Jungfrau, that travellers may rest themselves in its beauty, and watch for the avalanches that now and then come thundering down its precipitous sides. Streams of water are in some places pouring down. The music of the fall is constantly heard, and every five or ten minutes the roar of a snow-slide thunders on the ear. Few of them are seen. They break away from crags that are out of sight, and plunge into dark abysses where the eye of man does not follow them. But this is just the time of day when we might look for one, for it is past noon when the sun's power is the greatest, and if the great toppling mass which seems to be holding on with difficulty would but let go its cold death grasp and come headlong into this mighty grave at the base of the mountain, it would be a sight worth coming to Switzerland to see.

We watched and wished, and the more we watched, the more it would not come. During the half hour we had sat wrapped up in our blankets, gazing at the cold snow hills, and shivering in the bleak winds, the dinner had been in preparation, and despairing of getting something to see, we determined like sensible people, to have something to eat. The long table was filled with hungry travellers, and all had forgotten in the enjoyment of dinner the wonders of the Alps, when suddenly the alarm was given, " *Laweenen*," the " *Avalanche*." Servants dropped the dishes and ran, gentlemen and ladies following them rushed from the table, over chairs and each other, crowding for the doors and windows: and had there been danger of a sudden overwhelming of the house, and the destruction of all the inhabitants, we could not have fled in greater haste and confusion than we now did, to see the descending " thunderbolt of snow." All eyes were upon one point where a stream like powdered marble was pouring from one of the gullies far up the Jungfrau and lodging on a ledge. It differed in no respect from a stream of snow, nor indeed from one of water which is perfectly white in the distance when a small cascade is dangling from the rocks. Yet we are told, and there is no reason to doubt that this stream is made up of vast blocks of ice and masses of snow, dashed constantly into smaller fragments as it comes " rushing amain down," but still weighing each of them many tons, and capable of dealing destruction to forests and villages if they stood in its path. We looked on in silence, and with disappointment mingled with awe. The stream that had rested for a while on one ledge now began to flow again, and the roar of the torrent increased every instant, filling the air with its reverberations, which were caught by distant mountains and sent back in sharp echoes, and again in deep toned voices that seemed to shake the sky. But I was disappointed. It was just what I did not expect, although I had read enough of them to be prepared for what was to come. This was *said to be* one of the grandest scenes this season ! Of course we believed it, and report it accordingly. Grand indeed it was, and when we consider that at least four miles are between us and the hill side down which it is rushing, it is not surprising that the masses of ice should be blended into a steady and liquid stream. Certainly I prefer to see such a torrent at a distance, to being sufficiently near it to run any risk of being buried alive in an icy grave.

CHAPTER IX.

INTERLACHEN AND BERNE.

The Staubach Fall—Lauterbrunnen—Interlachen—Cretins and Goitre—Dr. Guggenbuhl—Giesbach Fall—Berne—Inquisitive Lady—Swiss Creed—Crossing the Gernmi—Leuchenbad Baths.

HE Staubach Fall, nearly a thousand feet high, is far from being such a thing of beauty as I had hoped to find it. It comes from such a height and has so small a body of water, that it dissolves into spray, and falling upon the rocks gathers itself up again and leaps down into the valley. Byron compares it to the tail of the white horse in the Apocalypse. Wordsworth speaks of it as a "heaven-born waterfall," and Murray likens it to a "beautiful lace veil suspended from a precipice." It is just at the

entrance of the village of Lauterbrunnen, which lies in a valley literally gloomy and sublime. The sides of the mountains that shut it in are precipitous and so lofty that in winter the sun does not climb the eastern side till noon, and so cold is it through the summer, that only the hardiest fruits can be raised. I counted between twenty and thirty cascades leaping over the brow of these mountains and plunging into the valley. In the calm of the evening, after the sun had ceased to shine in it, I rode from the village to Interlachen, and thought it the most mournfully pleasing ride in Switzerland. Others whom I met, and who passed me on the way, appeared to regard it as purely delightful, and perhaps few would find in it as I did, the materials of melancholy musings.

But all these feelings soon gave way to those of calm enjoyment, when a weary pilgrimage of a week was brought to a close in the beautiful village of INTERLACHEN.

We were at the hotel des Alpes; the largest and best boarding establishment in the village, where, for a dollar a day the traveller finds every comfort that a first class hotel affords. It was a very bright day, and the sun had been shining with a ravishing clearness on the snow-white breast of the Jungfrau. At the dinner-table, one of a party of ladies inquired the meaning of Jungfrau, and being told that it was German for a young unmarried lady, I ventured to say that it could not be called the Jungfrau to-morrow. "And why not, pray," was instantly demanded. "Because," said I, "she is certainly clad in her bridal robes to-day."

Beyond all doubt, it is the most beautiful single mountain in Switzerland. It is a calm, sweet pleasure to sit and look at her, as a bride adorned for her husband: white exceedingly; pure as the sun and snow; bright as the light, and glorious "as the gate of heaven." Sometimes its lofty summit seems to be touching the vault of heaven, and I could easily imagine that angels were on it, and not far from home. The wide plain in the midst of which the village is planted is the theatre of those yearly contests of strength and skill in which the inhabitants of all the surrounding hills and valleys engage. On the overhanging heights on your right hand as we go to Lauterbrunnen is the Castle of *Unspunnen*, to which a legend attaches that I have not time to tell. Byron is said to have had this scene before him when he made his Manfred. Instead of telling you the doubtful story of this old castle, I would rather give you some account of a modern and more humble house on the hill.

It is in sight from the plain: not an imposing struc-

ture, but so far above the vale, that you are tempted
to inquire what it is, and with a real pleasure you
are told it is Dr. Guggenbuhl's Asylum for Cretins.
For weeks we have been pained almost daily with
the sight of these miserable objects. More distressing to the eye is the victim of the *goitre*, which is a
swelling on the neck, gradually enlarging with the
growth of the unfortunate subject, till it hangs down
on the breast, and sometimes becomes so heavy that
the miserable individual is compelled to crawl on the
ground. What a strange ordering of Providence it is,
that these beautiful valleys should be infected with
such a disgusting disease. In the higher regions it is
not known, but in low, damp valleys where much
water remains stagnant, it abounds. And so de-
graded are many of the inhabitants, that some families regard it a blessing to have a case of goitre, as it
gives them a claim on the charity of others.

"Cretinism, which occurs in the same localities
as goitre, and evidently arises from the same cause,
whatever it may be, is a more serious malady, inas-
much as it affects the mind. The cretin is an idiot
— a melancholy spectacle — a creature who may
almost be said to rank a step below a human being.
There is a vacancy in his countenance; his head is
disproportionately large; his limbs are stunted or
crippled; he cannot articulate his words with dis-

8

tinctness; and there is scarcely any work which he is capable of executing. He spends his days basking in the sun, and, from its warmth, appears to derive great gratification. When a **stranger** appears, he becomes a clamorous and importunate beggar, assailing him with a ceaseless chattering; and the traveller is commonly glad to be rid of his hideous presence at the expense of a batz. At times the disease has such an effect on the mind, that the sufferer is unable to find his way home when within a few feet of his own door."

A young Swiss physician in Zurich, rapidly gaining fame and fortune in his profession, one day saw a little *cretin* near a fountain of water. His heart was touched with a sudden sympathy, not for the single unfortunate before him only, but for the thousands whom he knew to be scattered over his magnificent country. His noble heart was moved as he made an estimate of the numbers of his fellow beings in this helpless and now hopeless condition. In a single valley where some ten or fifteen thousand people live, not less than *three thousand* cretins are found. He could not redeem them all, but could he not do something for a few of them—put a new soul into these bodies—snatch them from the lower order of creation, from a lower level than the dog or the horse, and raise them to the scale of man? It was a noble impulse ; it was the beginning of a noble work. In the virtuous heroism of the hour, he resolved to give his life to the cause. Such a man could not have lived even a few years in a community without gaining the affections of all the good, and when it became known that the young physician would leave Zurich to study abroad the subject to which he had consecrated his powers, the poor people flocked about him, and held his knees beseeching him not to forsake them. But his resolution was taken.

His observation and study taught him that in the more elevated regions of the country, he would find the only place to locate a hospital, with any hope of making improvement in the miserable cases on whom he might make his experiments. Coming to this lovely vale of Interlachen, and selecting a lofty and most commanding site, away above the old castle of *Unspunnen*, with all the property that he possessed, and what he could obtain from the charity of those who were willing to aid him in his doubtful but philanthropic enterprise, he purchased a tract of mountain land, and built a house of refuge, a hospital for idiots.

I rode a donkey up the hill, and with my German friend Heinrich on one side of me, and my American friend Rankin on the other, we had a delightful excursion through the forest ; often emerging upon the

side of the hill from which we could look off on one
of the loveliest scenes, then winding our way by a
most circuitous and sometimes a very steep path, we
at last overcame the four miles of travel, and found
ourselves at the door of the Asylum. At our call a
young woman, evidently not a servant, came to the
door and showed us into a plainly furnished sitting
room, while she retired to announce to the Superin-
tendent that strangers would be pleased to view his
establishment. She returned with the register of vis-
iters in which we were desired to write our names
and address. She then carried the book to the Doctor, who soon appeared, gave us a cordial greeting,
and invited us to walk with him through the house.
While we had been sitting there, an uproar was going
on overhead, as if the floor was to be broken through.
Dr. Guggenbuhl led us directly to the room where the
riot was in progress. It was hushed as we entered.
But the cause was apparent. We were in the school-
room, and teachers and pupils were amusing themselves in the recess with all sorts of diverting and
boisterous plays. Here were thirty-seven idiots, of
various ages from three to thirty, in the way of being
trained to the first exercise of intelligent humanity,
the art of thinking. The teachers are young women,
the daughters of Swiss Protestant pastors chiefly, de-
voting themselves without fee or reward, like the Sis-

ters of Charity, to this painfully disagreeable task.
Around the room are hung large pictures of beasts
and birds, which are designed to catch the attention
of the cretins, and to induce them to make inquiries.
The first indication of a desire to know any thing is
seized upon with avidity and stimulated by every
encouragement. While we were standing there, several came in with one of the teachers from a ramble
in the woods. They had been for some years in training, and were now awake to the world around them.
They brought in beautiful wild flowers which they had
gathered, and were delighted to show to us, describing
their varieties, and exhibiting a familiarity with the
study that I did not dream of its being possible for
them to acquire. Feeble as were the exercises of
these poor things, it was a joy to know that they can
be taught, and Dr. G. assured me that he has had the
pleasure and reward of seeing some of them so far
restored to sense, that they may be expected to pro-
vide for themselves, and have some of the enjoyments
of rational beings. He is obliged to use his own
discretion in the admission of puplis : his house will
contain but his present number, and hundreds must
be denied his care, to whom he would gladly extend
it, if the rich would give him the means. He devotes
all his own property to their relief, and expects to
give his life to this self-denying work. In reply to my

inquiries if his labors were acknowledged by medical men abroad, he referred me to a score of diplomas that had been sent to him from all the leading Societies on the Continent of Europe and in England, but I saw none from America. **Does** not my country know, and does it not delight to honor a man whose philanthropy and **genius are alike** deserving the admiration of the world?

Among the poor idiots in this institution is one, the **son of an English Lord,** sent far away **from** his native land, in the hope, faint indeed, that the wonderful **skill** of this heroic man may open the eyes of this child's understanding. What indeed is wealth, and title, and power, to a fool? And O how happy they, who have joyous, bright and knowing little ones, though only bread and milk to eat, and little of that.

The good doctor followed us to the brow of the hill, and with us admired the lovely landscape away below, the richly tilled plain—the white cottages scattered over it, and in its midst the beautiful village—wide sheets of water around which the mountains stand and look down, solemn and grand, in their everlasting silence and gray heads: and then we pressed his hands long and earnestly, **asking God to** bless him, a noble specimen of a Christian physician.

While at Interlachen we made excursions to the Geisbach Falls, which have the preference in my view decidedly before all others in Switzerland. We also made a trip to Berne, and passed a few days at the *Couronne* Hotel, one of the best in the land.—Every body has read of the Bears of Berne, and there are many lions there to see, in the Museum and out. The view of the Bernese Alps is worth the journey to Switzerland. I saw them at sunset, in glory unrivalled and indescribable.

Returning from Berne in the diligence, an elderly English lady sitting in front of me, and hearing me converse with my friends, presumed I must be a countryman of her own, and opened a catechism as follows—

Lady.—" How long since you left England, Sir ?"

I.—About two months, Madam."

Lady.—" When do you return, Sir ?"

I.—I hope in the Spring, Madam.

Lady.—" Where do you spend the winter ?"

I.—In Syria.

Lady.—" Good Lord, what a traveller you are !"

She took a pinch of snuff, and I resumed my notes and remarks with my companion. She listened, and grew impatient to get hold of something by which to learn who we were. She at last ventured to come toward the point by asking,

" In what part of England do you reside, Sir ?"

I am not an Englishman, Madam.

Lady.—" Bless me, and of what country are you, pray ?"

I am an American.

Lady.—O you are, are **you** ? Well, I would not have thought it. Would it be an *indiscretion* for me to ask you what is your name, Sir ?"

I gave her my name of course, but she was not satisfied. " Will you," said she, " have the goodness to give me your name in writing ?"

I handed her my card, for which she thanked me, and then added, " I know that you are making notes, and will write a book, and I shall hear of you, &c.," and so she chatted on, amusing me not a little with her loquacity.

We returned to Interlachen, and here a German lady who was travelling with her family, begged me to allow her son, a student of Heidelberg, to join my party, to make an excursion of a few days, and meet her at Geneva. To this I assented, as it would increase our number to four, and be quite agreeable. With this escort of young men, two Germans and one American, I set off at daylight in the morning, to make the Gemmi Pass. Along the shores of Lake Thun and by the castles of Wimmis and of Spietz, we entered the beautiful vale of Frutigen, where the shepherds and flocks, with their crooks and their dogs, gave us a sweet picture of pastoral life. At a little

tavern at which we halted for lunch, I found the following CREED, framed and hung up in the dining-
room. It was in French.

" I believe in the Swiss country, the brave mother
of brave men, and in Freedom only begotten daugh-
ter of Helvetia, conceived in Grutli, by the patriot in
1308 who suffered under the aristocrats and priests,
was crucified for many centuries, died and was buried
in 1814; after sixteen years was again raised from
the dead, came back into the bosom of true patriots,
from hence she shall come to judge all the wicked. I
believe in the human spirit which was delivered from
ignorance by knowledge and raised by Education. I
believe in a holy general brotherhood of the oppressed
in Spain, Portugal, Poland and Italy, the communion
of all patriots, the destruction of all tariffs, and the
life everlasting of republics, Amen."

This is scarcely better than blasphemy; and it is
probably one of the formulas of faith on which the
Continental conspiracies are formed. On and up, the
road led us to some beautiful falls of water, and between perpendicular masses of rock that stood as if
split asunder to give us a passage through. We
reached Kanderstey in the middle of the day, and
met parties returning from the Gemmi, who advised
us against going on, as there was every prospect of a

coming storm. We were determined however to
press forward. I got a mule and a guide, and the
young men were ready to walk. We set off in good
spirits, but as soon as we struck into the defile which
led up the hill, the mists began to thicken around us,
and it was impossible to call it any thing but rain.
Three hours of steady climbing brought us to the
wretched inn of Schwarenbach, which Werner makes
the scene of a fearful tale of blood. We were wet
and cold, but found no fire, and the set of men and
women inside were too dirty and savage to tempt us
to spend the night with them, as we were now heartily
disposed to do, if the quarters had been safe. I preferred to run the risk of getting over the mountain to
staying here. This was the unanimous vote, and
again we plunged into the storm. Dreary and dismal
was the way, along by the side of the Lake; the Dau-
ben See, and in the midst of broken masses of stone,
strewed in wild disorder. We were near the summit
when the rain became snow and hail, and the winds
swept fearfully over us, so that I could not sit upon
my mule. I had scarcely dismounted, before he
slipped on a ledge and fell; I might have broken my
neck had I fallen with him. No signs of a human
habitation are on this lonely height. And if there
were, we could not find them in this driving storm.
There are no monks to come with their dogs to look

us up, if we lose the way. We must go over and down on the other side, or perish. To return is impossible. Among the scattered fragments of rocks, no path was to be seen; and we frequently feared that we had lost our way. I followed the guide to the brink of a precipice two thousand feet deep, and perpendicular. Down the face of this solid rock leads the most wonderful of all the pathways in Switzerland. So narrow as just to allow two mules to pass as they meet, the zigzag path is cut out of the solid rock, and covered with earth and stones to prevent our feet from slipping. The mule, by a wonderful instinct, walks upon the extreme outer verge, lest in making the sudden turn his load should strike the rock and tumble him off.

Sheltered somewhat from the rain by the overhanging rocks, we pursued our weary way to the bottom; and then, through mud and mire and darkness, drenched to our skins, we reached the Hotel Blanche at Leukenbad.

This is the great bathing establishment of Switzerland. It is higher above the sea than the summit of any mountain in Great Britain. Again and again it has been swept away by avalanches, and is now protected by a strong wall above the village. The water bursts out from the ground immediately in front of our hotel, and supplies the baths, which are twenty feet square, and in which a dozen or twenty men and women may be seen, for hours, sitting with their heads only out of water, reading the newspapers, or books, on little floats before them ; playing chess ; or whiling away the time in some more agreeable manner.

The next morning, by a most romantic pathway along the borders of a vast abyss, the scene of a bloody battle in 1799, we pursued our journey to the valley of the Rhone, and taking the Great Simplon road, through Sion, went to Martigny.

CHAPTER X.

MONKS OF SAINT BERNARD.

The Char-a-banc—the Napoleon Pass—Travellers in winter—Monks—Dogs—Dinner—Music—Dead-house—Contributions—a Monk's Kiss.

HE weather was threatening when we set off from Martigny, and we had many forebodings that the dogs of Saint Bernard might have to look us up, if the storm should come before we reached the hospice. A char-a-banc, a narrow carriage in which we sat three in a line with the *tandem* horses, was to convey us to the village of Liddes. On leaving the valley and crossing the river Drance, we soon commenced the ascent, by the side of the raving torrent, with majestic heights on either hand. A terrible tale of devastation

(181)

and misery, of sublime fortitude and heroic courage, is told of the valley of Bagnes, where the ice had made a mighty barrier against the descending waters, which accumulated so rapidly that a lake seven thousand feet wide was formed, and a tunnel was cut through the frozen dam with incredible toil, when it burst through and swept madly over the country below, bearing destruction upon its bosom. In two hours some four hundred houses were destroyed with thirty-four lives and half a million dollars' worth of property. We were four hours and a half getting up to Liddes, where we had a wretched dinner, and then mounted horses to ride to the summit of the pass.

The rain, which had been falling at intervals all the morning, was changed into snow as we got into colder regions. The path became rougher and more difficult, and it was hard to believe that even the indomitable spirit of Napoleon could have carried an army with all the munitions of war, over such a route as this. Yet the passage now is smooth and easy compared with what it was when in 1800 he crossed the Alps.

Leaving the miserable village of Saint Pierre, through which a Roman Catholic procession was passing, we had an opportunity of refusing to take off our hats, though some of the peasants insisted on our so doing. We came up to heights where no trees

THE HOSPICE OF ST. BERNARD.

and few shrubs were growing : flowers would sometimes put their sweet faces up through the snow and
smile on us as we passed, and I stopped to gather
them as emblems of beauty and happiness in the
midst of desolation and death.

The most of the travellers on their upward way,
were mounted on mules, but a few were on foot, and
among these was one of the monks of the Hospice,
who with a couple of blooming Swiss damsels, was
returning to his quarters from a visit below. We
passed one or two cottages, and a house of stone
which has been built away up here for the reception
of benighted travellers, and after a toilsome journey
of four hours, just at sunset we came upon the Hospice, a large three-story stone house, on the height of
the mountain more than eight thousand feet above
the sea, the highest inhabited spot in Europe. To
shelter those who are compelled to cross this formida-
ble pass in winter, when the paths are far down
underneath the snow, and travellers are in danger of
being overtaken by storms, or overcome with fatigue
and sinking in the depths of the drifts, this *hospice*
has been founded and sustained. In the summer
season, as now, it is merely a large hotel, where pleasure parties are drawn by curiosity to visit the monks
and their establishment, famed the world over for its
hospitality and self-denying charity. The snow was

falling fast as we ascended the rugged pass, and at
least six inches of it lay on the ground at the top. I
was glad to have reached it, in the midst of such a
storm. It gave me a vivid picture of the hospice
when its walls and cheerful fires and kind sympathies
are needed for worn and exhausted pilgrims. Such
were some who arrived here this evening. Father
Maillard, a young monk, received us at the door, and
after pleasing salutations conducted us to our chambers, plainly furnished apartments with no carpets on
the floor, but with good beds. The house was very
cold. As the season is not yet far advanced, perhaps
their winter fires were not kindled, and as no fuel is
to be had except what is brought up from below on
the backs of horses, it is well for the monks to be
chary of its use. Our host led us to the chamber in
which Napoleon slept when he was here, and my
young German friend occupied the same bed in
which the Emperor lay. He did not tell me in the
morning that his dreams were any better than mine,
though I had but a humble pilgrim's.

After we had taken possession of our quarters, we
were at liberty to survey the establishment. We
began at the kitchen, where a small army of servants
were preparing dinner, over immense cooking stoves.
The house is fitted up to lodge seventy guests, but
oftentimes a hundred and even five hundred have

been known to be here at one time. To get dinner
for such a host, in a house so many miles above
the rest of the world, is no small affair. We came
up to the Cabinet, enriched with a thousand curious
objects of nature and art, many of them presented by
travellers grateful for kindness they had received, and
some of them relics of the old Romans who once had
a temple to Jupiter on this spot. The reception
room, which was also a sitting and dining room,
was now rapidly filling up with travellers, arriving
at nightfall. One English lady, overcome with
the exertion of climbing the hill on horseback,
sank upon the floor and fainted as soon as she was
brought in. A gentleman who had but little more
nerve in him, was also exhausted. The kind-hearted
priests hastened to bring restoratives, and speedily
carried off the invalids to their beds—the best place
for them. It was quite late, certainly seven in the
evening before dinner was served, and with edged
appetites, such as only mountain climbing in snow
time can set, we were ready at the call. The monks
wait upon their guests, girded with a napkin, taking
the place of servants, and thus showing, or making a
show of humility. It was not pleasant to my feelings
to have a St. Augustine monk, in the habit of his
order, a black cloth frock reaching to his feet, and
buttoned, with a white band around his neck, and

passing down in front and behind to his girdle, now
standing behind me while I was eating, offering
to change my plate, and serving me with an alacrity
worth imitating by those whose businesss it is to wait
on table.   And when I said, " thank you, father," in
Italian, it was no more than the tribute of respect
due to a gentleman of education and taste, whose
religion had condemned him to such a life as this.
Father Maillard presided at the table, and was very
conversable with the guests; cheerfully imparting
such information as we desired.   Of the eight or ten
monks here, not one of then speaks the English language ; but the French, Italian and German are all in
use among them.   I inquired of Father Maillard if
those terrible disasters of which we formerly read so
much, travellers perishing in the snow, are of frequent occurrence in late years.   He told me that
rarely, I think he said never, does a winter pass,
without some accident of the sort.   Hundreds of the
peasantry, engaged in trade, or for the sake of visiting friends, will make the pass, and though the paths
are marked by high poles set up in Summer, these
are sometimes completely buried under mountains of
snow, and the poor traveller loses his way and sinks
as he would in the sea.   He also told me that after
his brethren reside in this cold climate for a few
years, they find their health giving way and they are

obliged to retire to some other field of labor, and usually with broken constitutions. Yet there are always some who are willing, at this hazard, to devote the best years of their life to the noble work of saving the lives of others. Honor to the men, whether their faith be ours or not.

Our dinner, this being our only dinner where monks were our hosts and servants, is worth being reported. We had no printed bill of fare; but my young friends helped me to make one out the next day as follows: 1. Vermicelli soup. 2. Beef a la mode. 3. Potatoes. 4. Roast Lamb. 5. Roast Veal stuffed. 6. Dessert of nuts, figs, cheese, &c. This with plenty of wine, for which the cellars of St. Bernard are famous, was dinner and supper enough for any, certainly we were prepared to do it justice, as to a table spread in the wilderness.

After dinner, the party now numbering fifty or more, assembled from the two or three refectories, in the drawing-room, and the many languages spoken gave us a small idea of Babel. One of the priests took his seat at a poor piano, sadly out of tune; and commenced playing some lively airs. The two Swiss maidens who had come up with him to visit the hospice, stood one on each side of him, at the piano, and sang with great glee to his music, and at the close of every song, the party applauded with hearty clapping of hands, that would have pleased Mario and Grisi. I asked Father Maillard, who stood by me all the evening, **and with whom I** formed a very pleasant acquaintance, if they had such gay times every night. He said that during the summer travel **they had** many pleasant people who enjoyed themselves much during their brief visit. We certainly **did.** And at an hour later than usual we retired to **our** chambers. It was so cold that I had to take my Glasgow blanket **and wrap myself well up in it** before **turning in, but I slept** soundly, **and was awakened** by the Convent bell, before daylight, calling the monks to morning prayers. I rose, and hastily dressing, hurried to the chapel. The priests, the servants, and thirty or forty muleteers who had come with the travellers were on their knees on the stone floor of a **pretty little chapel,** devoutly worshipping. None of the travellers were here : but those who entertained and served them, had left their beds before dawn to pray.

Breakfast was not prepared for **all at once, but** each person as he was ready called for his coffee and rolls, and they were immediately **brought.**

The celebrated **dogs of** St. Bernard were playing **in** the snow as I stepped out after breakfast : a noble set of fellows they were, and invested with a sort of romantic nobility, when we thought **of them plough-**

ing their way through drifts, leading on the search for lost travellers, and carrying on their necks a basket of bread and wine which may be as life to the dead.

The dead! Come and see them. Close by the hospice is a square stone house, into which are carried the lifeless bodies of those who perish in the snow, and are found by the dogs, or on the melting of the snow in the summer. They cannot dig graves on these rocky heights, and it is always so cold that the bodies do not rot, but they are placed in this charnel-house just as they are found, and are left to dry up and gradually to turn to dust. I counted thirty skulls lying on the ground in the midst of ribs, arms and legs; and twenty skeletons were standing around the sides of the room, a ghastly sight. In one corner a dead mother held the bones of her dead child in her arms: as she perished so she stood, to be recognized if it might be, by anxious friends, but none had ever come to claim her. What a tale of tender and tragic interest, we read in these bones. Sad, and sickening the sight is, and I am willing to get away.

Father Maillard walked with me into the chapel, showed me the paintings, and the monument of Gen. DESSAIX, and when I asked him for the box into which alms are put, he pointed to it, and hastened

away that he might not see what I put in. They
make no charge for entertaining travellers, but every
honest man will give at least as much in the way of a
donation as he would pay at a hotel.

My friend, as I now call him, Father Maillard,
embraced me tenderly, and even kissed me, when I
bade him farewell, and mounting my horse, set off
at eight in the morning, with a bright sunshine, to
descend the mountain.

CHAPTER XI.

FIRST SIGHT OF MONT BLANC.

The Host of Martigny—Vale of the Drance—Mount Rosa—Tete Noire—Col de Balm—The Monarch of the Alps.

RING me for my ride to-morrow the *easiest* of all the mules in Martigny," I said to Antonio, on the evening after my return from the pass of St. Bernard. I was knocked up nearly, done over certainly, and contemplated another trip with a sort of shrink. But there is nothing in Martigny to see, after you have looked at the measures of the various heights to which the water has risen in times of inundation, to which these valley-villages are sadly subject. So in the morning— a bright glad day it was—Antonio came in to tell me

(193) 9

that he had a lady's mule for me, so easy I should be
in danger of falling asleep on his back; but this hazard I was willing to risk. The past few days of walking and riding had made me so stiff in the joints that
I was awkward about mounting, and my host of the
Poste, a huge man as well as an admirable publican,
put his hands under my shoulders, and with all ease
placed me astride of the beast in a moment. The
feat was received with applause by a score of rough-
looking peasants, guides, beggars, &c., of whom there
are plenty in this unwholesome valley; and we were
off for the vale of CHAMOUNI.

Following up the river Drance, we turned off to
the right, and slowly worked our way by a bad pathway, meeting people now and then coming down
with their truck to sell below. One man had a log
of wood with a string tied around it, dragging it
behind him, women with baskets of knick-knacks, all
intent upon driving a trade in a very small way, but
industriously, and that commends a people to you
wherever you see them. On the left were terrible
precipices, along the edge of which the path often
led us; till we came to a lovely reach of pasturages,
a wide plain where cottages were scattered, and
flocks were grazing—a peaceful scene in the midst
of rugged mountains. Crossing this plain we ascended the Forclaz, and from the ridge looked back

on the valley of the Rhone.   The great road over
the Simplon stretches for many a long mile up this
vale, and Sion in the distance is seen; and around
us more than fifty snowy peaks of the Alps with the
morning sun gilding their crowns.   Among them,
but in beauty above them all is Mount Rosa, admired
even more than Mont Blanc; and now that peculiar
tint of pink was spread all over it with uncommon
lustre.   " Great glory " was the exclamation which
often rose to my lips as from one and another point
of observation I looked at these white mountains,
and the " excessive brightness " blazing from every
summit.   But we cannot always be on the mountain
tops looking at still higher mountains.   We descend
into the valley of Trient, into which a glacier extends,
bringing its perpetual ice into the bosom of a sweet
vale, where green meadows were rejoicing, and the
peasants were busy with a scant harvest.

We have our choice of two roads from this valley
to Chamouni.   The one by the *Tete Noire* is the easi-
est, and we resolved in the freshness of our strength
to take this road first, and having pursued it to the
Tete, to enjoy the view, and then come back and go
by the Col de Balm.   By this extra effort we accomplished a noble day's work, and were richly repaid for
the fatigue.   In no part of Switzerland are the precipices grander and more fearful, and for an hour we

rode along the edge; and when the rocks shoot out over the path, a tunnel or gallery as they call it, is cut through; and near by a rude inscription cut into the rock celebrates an English lady who contributed something to improve the pass. The *Tete* or Head, Black Head, is given to the dark mountain, whose overhanging rocks present a gloomy front which has given its name to this narrow defile. Hundreds of feet down in the dark abyss on whose verge we are travelling, the Trient is roaring and leaping along its rocky way to the Rhone. At every turn in our zig-zag single-file march, we are tempted to pause and study the scenes of sublime and terrible that break upon us: for when we are in no danger ourselves, there is a fascination in looking upon scenes where the fearful makes us shudder. But we returned from these out-of-the-way places and were at noon in the valley of Trient again, gazing at the lofty crags from which Escher de Berg fell in 1791, when, like many more fortunate travellers, he disregarded the advice of his guides, and lost his life in showing his temerity and strength in making a leap.

The ascent of the Col de Balm has been described by the most of travellers as one of the most difficult, and we are told it seems incredible that mules can work their way up where travellers are obliged to climb by the roots and shrubs. But over this hill lies the road to Chamouni, and over this hill we are going. For an hour we did have hard work, and Heinrich and I amused ourselves with digging up some Greek roots, while the mules were slowly picking their way among the stones up a path sometimes all but perpendicular. And when at last we emerged from the forest, and reached the high pasturages, we had still a long hour of travel before us, through the open country.

Our party had been enlarged during the morning by the accession of others on the same route, and as we were nearing the ridge, there began to be quite a strife among us as to whose eyes should have the first sight of Mont Blanc. For a month we had been on and under the mountains of Switzerland; gazing successively upon higher and yet higher heights; and when the Jungfrau, and Mount Rosa, and other of the lesser kings of the country had stood before us, we could not believe that any other could be a monarch in the midst of such mountains as these. But Mont Blanc was always to come. It was the last, for we had seen them all, rejoiced in them all, looked up through them all to Him who holds them in his hand, and counts them only as dust in the balance; and still one more wonderful than they was just before us, on the other side of the ridge, and in a few moments more would stand up and meet us face to face.

Over the pasturages there were many paths, and we scattered in our attempts to gain upon each other. The mules seemed to catch somewhat of the inspiration of the occasion, and did their best, till we came out together, neck and neck, and we stood on the summit, with the vale of Chamouni, the steeple-like *Aiguilles* of Charmoz and Midi, Argentiere and Verte, and others shooting up cold and black, sentinels around the hoary old monarch of the Alps lying there with a crown of mist on his head, which rises as we look at it, and Mont Blanc is before us.

"Disappointed of course," you say. Perhaps so. It does not stand in the middle of a plain, and rise right up like a pyramid, till its apex touches the blue sky. In fact, you must be assured by your guide that the round summit to the South of two or three that seem to be higher is actually Mont Blanc, the loftiest of them all; and as you sit here and take in the wonderful panorama of the glaciers, needles, and majestic summits, the grandeur gradually steals into your soul and takes quiet possession. I wanted to be still and absorb the scene, which I should soon leave and never see again. I would expose my heart to it, till a sort of daguerreotype was made, which I could carry with me, and look at when I should sit down at Niagara, or among the White Hills of New Hampshire.

CHAMOUNI AND MT. BLANC.

"'Pon my honor, 'tis very fine," said a very red-faced, red-whiskered Englishman, who had followed me to my solitary stand-point. "What do you think of it? Is it not fine: very fine?" And so he kept chattering on, till I crept off gently a few rods, and again essayed to be alone. But my tormentor followed up, and renewed his attack, as if it were impossible for him to see the prospect with any satisfaction unless he could keep talking to somebody all the while. A small house of entertainment stands here, and while my Englishman went in to have some brandy and water, I managed to get a few moments of undisturbed possession of the scene. Of all the points of observation in this country of stupendous scenes, there is no one that furnishes a more sublime and glorious spectacle than this. It is the crowning hour of the tour of Switzerland. I felt that I had reached the climax, and with reverence I could make a parody on the words of old Simeon. All my feelings have been of reverence in this country. The Alps and God have been around me for a month, and my soul has been rising in high converse with Him who covers these hills with his presence, and is glorious in the solitudes of these vales. And now as I look off at these glistening glaciers, so many miles of resplendent ice, a *Mer de Glace*, a sea of glass, lying among those mountains, and extending far down into

the vales below ; when I look up at these precipitous
peaks actually piercing the clouds, and then at the
solemn brows of those giant mountains, where the
foot of man has seldom trod, and the glory of God is
forever shining, I feel a sense of the presence of the
Infinite and Eternal as no other scene has ever yet
awakened in my soul. With the disciples on another
Mount, I feel " it is good to be here."

That was my first sight of Mont Blanc. The day
could not have been more favorable, and that evening
as the sun went down, I stood in the vale of Chamouni
and saw his last rays lingering on the summit, the
stars trooping around it at night, and the next morning before sunrise I was out again to see the first
beams of day as they kissed his brow.

> Awake, my soul ! not only passive praise
> Thou owest ; not alone these swelling tears,
> Mute thanks and secret ecstacy ! Awake,
> Voice of sweet song ! Awake, my heart, awake !
> Green vales and icy cliffs, all join my hymn.—
> Thou first and chief, sole sovereign of the vale !
> O struggling with the darkness all the night,
> And visited all night by troops of stars,
> Or when they climb the sky, or when they sink ;
> Companion of the morning-star at dawn,
> Thyself earth's rosy star, and of the dawn
> Co-herald ! wake, O ! wake, and utter praise !
> Who sank thy sunless pillars deep in earth ?
> Who filled thy countenance with rosy light ?
> Who made thee parent of perpetual streams ?
> And you, ye five wild torrents fiercely glad,

Who called you forth from night and utter death,
From dark and icy caverns called you forth,
Down those precipitous, black, jagged rocks,
Forever shattered, and the same forever?
Who gave you your invulnerable life,
Your strength, your speed, your fury, and your joy,
Unceasing thunder, and eternal foam?
And who commanded, (and the silence came,)
" Here let the billows stiffen, and have rest?"—
Ye ice-falls! ye that from the mountain's brow
Adown enormous ravines slope amain!
Torrents, methinks, that heard a mighty voice,
And stopped at once amid their maddest plunge!
Motionless torrents! silent cataracts!
Who made you glorious as the gates of heaven
Beneath the keen full moon? Who bade the sun
Clothe you with rainbows? Who, with living flowers
Of loveliest hue, spread garlands at your feet?
God! Let the torrents, like a shout of nations,
Answer, and the ice-plains echo, God!—
God! sing ye meadow-streams with gladsome voice!
Ye pine-groves, with your soft and soul-like sounds!
And they too have a voice, yon piles of snow,
And in their perilous fall shall thunder, God!—
Ye living flowers that skirt the eternal frost,
Ye wild-goats sporting round the eagle's nest,
Ye eagles, playmates of the mountain storm,
Ye lightnings, the dread arrows of the clouds,
Ye signs and wonders of the element,
Utter forth, God! and fill the hills with praise.—
Once more, hoar mount, with thy sky-pointing peaks,
Oft from whose feet the avalanche, unheard,
Shoots downward glittering through the pure serene,
Into the depth of clouds that veil thy breast.—
Thou too, again, stupendous mountain thou
That, as I raise my head, awhile bowed low
In adoration upward from thy base,
Slow travelling, with dim eyes suffused with tears,

Solemnly seemest, like a vapory cloud,
To rise before me,—rise, O ! ever rise,
Rise like a cloud of incense, from the earth !
Thou kingly spirit throned-among the hills,
Thou dread ambassador from earth to heaven.
Great hierarch ! tell thou the silent sky,
And tell the stars, and tell yon rising sun,
Earth, with her thousand voices, praises God.

CHAPTER XII.

A good House—Prisoner of Chillon—Calvin—Dr. Malan—Dr. Gaussen—Col.
Tronchin—The Cemetery.

 56 **M**hHotel *des Bergues* stands on
the Lake of Geneva, just where the
" arrowy Rhone" shoots out from
its bosom. This is one of the finest
hotels in Europe, and with the
Trois Couronnes at Vevay, may
fairly challenge comparison with
any other. I brought up at this
house from the Vale of Chamouni.
The dismal rain through which I had been riding on
a chill autumn day, had increased to a storm, and the
old town, that is gloomy enough at any time, was
peculiarly uninviting on its first appearance. But

(205)

this city I had longed to visit, even from the time that I read in Cæsar's Commentaries, " the farthest town of the Allobroges and the nearest to the frontier of the Helvetii, is GENEVA." Julius Cæsar took possession of it, and the remains of his erections are to be seen at the present day.

The Christian religion was introduced in the fifth century, and bishops appointed by the Pope by degrees became lords temporal as well as spiritual, which they are very apt to do as fast and as far as they can get the power. The right of naming the Bishops, about the year 1400, fell into the hands of the ducal house of Savoy, and their creatures became despots of the reddest dye. Their oppressions grew to be so intolerable that the citizens rebelled. A bloody persecution ensued. The chapter of its history is among the darkest of the records of popery. The deeds of patriotic heroism which were brought out have scarcely a parallel. One citizen cut his own tongue out with a razor, lest the torture should compel him to betray his friends. Bonnivard became the chained prisoner of Chillon. But his story is not to be passed over without being told.

" In 1530, *Francois Bonnivard*, *Prior of Saint Victor*, was seized on the Jorat by a band of marauders, whose chief was the Sieur de Beaufort, Governor

of Chillon, for his bitter enemy, the Duke of Savoy.
As a punishment for his heroic defence of the liberty
of Geneva, he was condemned by the petty tyrant to
perpetual captivity in the castle. Here he remained
during seven years, buried alive in a dungeon on a
level with the waters of the lake, and fastened by a
chain round his body to a ring still remaining on one
of the pillars. Irritated to agony by sad reflections
on his own and his adopted country's slavery, he
wore away the stone floor beneath his feet, by constantly pacing to and fro, like a wild beast, from end
to end of its cage. At length, in 1536, the Bernese,
with their allies of Geneva, effected the conquest of
the Pays du Vaud. Chillon was the last place which
held out for Duke Charles V. of Savoy, but the Bernese having laid siege to it by land, while the Genevese gave an assault by water, the garrison was
forced to a surrender, and Bonnivard, with several
other prisoners, was restored to liberty. He had left
Geneva a Roman Catholic state, under the domination
of the House of Savoy, he found her a free republic,
openly professing the reformed religion. The citizens
were by no means backward in recompensing him for
past sufferings; in June, 1536, he was admitted to
the highest privileges of the State, and presented with
the house previously inhabited by the Roman Catholic Vice-General, besides an annual pension of two

hundred crowns of gold, so long as he chose to dwell there."

Then came the Reformation. The people, long sick of Roman despotism and disgusted with Romish wickedness, embraced the doctrines of the Reformers, and Geneva became doubly free. John Calvin came in 1536, and Protestants from other countries fled to Geneva as an asylum from persecution. His genius and austere morals, contrasted with the dissoluteness of the Romish Clergy, gave him unbounded influence in the state. He was called the Pope, and Geneva the Rome of Protestantism. John Knox was here with him, and hundreds of distinguished men whose principles made it necessary for them to fly from England, France, Spain and Italy. Through the seventeenth century the city had rest, and made great progress in arts and science; the resort of men of learning, and distinguished for the industry and thrift of its inhabitants. The eighteenth century was marked with insurrections, distractions, civil wars and revolution. The scenes of Paris were performed in Geneva. The blood of her best citizens was shed by the hands of the mob, in the name of liberty. Then the city was grafted upon France, and so remained till 1813, when with the aid of Austria, it became once more a Genevan Republic. The next

year it became one of the Cantons of Switzerland,
but the city held on to its aristocratic constitution.
Still it flourished in peace and progress, till the con-
test between the radical and conservative parties
broke out in 1841, and resulted in the revision of the
constitution, but not in the establishment of confi-
dence and quiet. In 1846 a fierce struggle occurred,
still fresh in every memory, which ended in the
establishment of the present constitution, on a democratic basis, and in giving an impulse to the attempt
to overturn the thrones of despotism in Europe; a
noble but abortive effort, which failed in 1848.
Geneva, under John Calvin, called Europe to religious liberty in 1536, and the people heard the call.
If another John Calvin had been in Geneva in 1848,
we should not have been compelled to deplore the
miscarriage of that struggle in Europe for Constitu-
tional liberty, which shook every government, but
eventuated in giving a charter to the people of but a
single State.

I had been wandering a month among the mountains of Switzerland, and had not had a line from
home. The bankers closed their offices at four
o'clock and it was nearly five when we arrived.
Disappointed and grieved I returned to the Hotel,
the more sad as to-morrow is to be the Sabbath, and
I shall not be able to get my letters till Monday. It

occurred to me that something might have been sent
for me to the care of a venerable and well-known
clergyman of Geneva, whom I should not fail to see,
and I would therefore call at once upon him, without
ceremony. I soon found his gate. A woman at the
lodge answered the bell and took my card up to the
house with a message to ask if anything had been
left for me; for it was late and Saturday evening,
and I would not intrude upon the pastor at such an
hour. In a few moments the good man stood on the
walk, under the trees, with a lantern in his hand; a
tall old man, with long grey hair hanging in curls,
and a countenance shining with love. He put out
his hands and throwing one arm around me drew me
to him, as if I were his only son, and kissed me. It
was the Rev. Dr. CÆSAR MALAN, and a welcome such
as a pilgrim in a strange land can feel. Many
pleasant hours I had with his interesting family, now
reduced by the frequent inroads which my countrymen have made upon it. No less than three of them
have repaid this good man's hospitality by carrying
off his daughters; and the last but one had been
taken but a few days before I arrived. These deeds
were done by clergymen from America, and when I
was asked in a social gathering of Genevan ladies, if
my countrymen were obliged to go abroad for their
wives, I could only say that no one would blame them

for taking a wife at a venture when they come to Geneva.

The gentle GAUSSEN, author of an excellent work on the Inspiration of the Scriptures, charmed me with his sweet Christian spirit, and his broad-hearted charity, so happily in contrast with much of the foreign half-reformed religion, which in England and France still abounds. D'Aubigne was not at home.

Col. Tronchin has a lovely residence out of town and overlooking the lake. He sustains at his own charges an asylum for convalescing invalids, one of the most interesting charities I have ever seen. He took me through the establishment, and I felt, as I never did before, what a blessedness it is to have wealth and a heart to use it for the sake of those who are suffering. A young woman sitting at the door and enjoying the sunshine, pale and thin, but smiling with the prospect of returning health, rose, when he stopped and asked her if she was getting well, and blessed him for her comforts, with looks and words of gratitude that must have been a rich reward. This home for the poor is charmingly situated in the midst of shade-trees, with walks and beds of flowers, and furnished with everything to promote the health and comfort of the patients, who come here when discharged from the hospitals as no longer requiring medical aid, and are yet unable to labor. In the pure air of this rural abode, and surrounded with all all the good things which this benevolent man has provided, twenty-five invalids are supported at his expense, and as soon as one departs, another is ready and waiting to come in. Indeed it occurred to me that many of them would be slow to get well if they must be banished from this lovely spot to a cellar or garret in ·a crowded street, to toil and sicken again.

Begging in the streets is forbidden, and in the whole of Switzerland you may distinguish between the Protestant and Catholic cantons, by the fact that few beggars are in the former, compared with the crowds that infest the latter, annoying and often disgusting the traveller. The morals of the two religions are as strikingly contrasted. The Catholics accuse the Genevese females of prudery, and Sismondi tells us that the young women are " pious, well brought up, prudent and good managers."

In the cemetery I found the grave of Sir Humphrey Davy and Pictet and other distinguished men, foreigners and citizens, but no man knows where Calvin is buried. He forbade any monument to be erected to mark the spot, and so it has passed from the knowledge of man. But in the old cathedral, standing on the spot where once stood a pagan temple of Apollo, is the pulpit in which Calvin and Knox and Beza, Farel and Viret, and a long line of glorious men, have preached : and this noble building, presenting many fine specimens of architecture and sculpture of the middle ages, now wrested from the hands of Popery, is a fitting monument to the memory of the Reformers. In the public library founded by *Bonnivard*, the Prisoner of Chillon, I saw the manuscripts and portraits of all the Genevan Reformers, four hundred of the MSS. being Calvin's, and a collection of literary curiosities of unrivalled interest. There is little else to see in Geneva. Its attraction lies in its historic interest, its delightful situation, and good society. In and around it, all along the borders of Lake Leman, are sites made famous by the residence of men and women of taste and letters.

CHAPTER XIII.

PICTURES IN SWITZERLAND.*

Waterfalls—Constance—Zurich—William Tell—Glaciers—the Monarch.

HE waterfalls of Switzerland are among its crowning glories ; and of these the falls of Schaffhausen are altogether the most imposing. The European, who has never worshiped at the foot of our own great cataract, looks down from the base of the Castle of Lauffen, after paying a franc for the privilege of getting to a standing-place ; or he looks up from the opposite shore, where is reared the Castle of Worth, and he pronounces it magnificent. Mrs. Bull does not hesi-

* The preceding letters were originally addressed to the New York Observer. This chapter, embracing a general view of the country, with pictures of scenes already noticed, was contributed to Harper's Monthly Magazine.

(214)

tate to declare it charming! Mr. Murray, in that
everlasting Red book, without which no Englishman
could *do* Europe—as this is the authority on which
alone he ventures to admire any thing in art or
nature, just as he swears only by the *Times*—Mr.
Murray, in his never-to-be-dispensed-with Hand-book,
informs him that this is " the finest cataract in
Europe," and, of course, in his opinion, it is the finest
in the world. He leads the trembling traveller to
the verge of the awful precipice, where, covered with
spray, he may enjoy the full grandeur of this " hell
of waters," and then he adds, " It is only by this close
proximity, amidst the tremendous roar and the unin-
terrupted rush of the river, that a true notion can be
formed of the stupendous nature of this cataract!"
The Rhine here leaps over the rocks into an abyss of
fifty feet. The river is cloven in twain by a tower of
rock in the centre of the stream, and the spray rises
from its base in an eternal cloud. Picturesque and
beautiful the falls certainly are, but grandeur can
hardly be affirmed of them.

It was my first day of travel in Switzerland when
I reached them—a warm day in the summer of last
year. A month of hot weather in Dresden and
Munich had been too much for the restoring powers
of the waters of Baden-Baden, and it was like waking
up in a new world of beauty, with a new soul to love

it, to find myself in the midst of this Swiss scenery—
the breezes of its snow hills and glaciers fanning me,
and its peaks pointing skyward, where there are tem-
ples and palaces whose every dome is a sun and every
pinnacle a star.   But I could not be satisfied till,
with the aid of two stout fellows, I made my way
through the boiling waters nearly to the foot of the
central tower, and there, in the toppling skiff which
threatened to tip over on very gentle occasions, I
looked up at the mass of waters tumbling from above.
The rocks were partially covered with green shrubbery, and a scraggy tree stretched its frightful arms
into the spray ; but I was not disposed to climb, as
some have done, to the top of the cliff, for the sake of
enjoying the scene.

A curious old town is Schaffhausen, so named from
the boat-houses, or skiff-houses, which were here
erected, for the falls made this the great terminus of
navigation on the Rhine.   We had come by diligence
from Basle, and after passing a night in Weber's
excellent hotel at the falls, we came on in the morning, and spent an hour or two looking at the ancient
architecture of the town, whose buildings are adorned
with such fanciful and extravagant carvings as would
hardly be deemed ornamental in the Fifth Avenue.

A very small specimen of a steamer received us
now, and bore us up against a strong current.   The

banks on either side were green with vineyards, now loaded with unripe fruit, and in the midst of the vines the dressers were at their work. On the sloping hillsides the neat cottages of the Swiss peasantry were scattered, making a picture of constant beauty through which we were passing. Among our passengers were a dozen German students, with their knapsacks on their backs, making a tour of Switzerland, the most of which they would perform on foot, gathering health and strength as they trudged on through the mountain passes, and studied the glacier theories on the spot.

It was noon when we arrived at Constance, on the lake of the same name, and a city to be forever associated with the trial and martyrdom of John Huss and Jerome of Prague—a city on which the curse of shedding innocent blood seems resting to this day. In the loft of a long building, now standing near the water's edge, was gathered a Council, in the year of our Lord 1414, over which the Emperor Sigismund presided, and attended by some five hundred princes, cardinals, bishops, archbishops and professors, who deposed two popes and set up another, and crowned their four years' labor of love by condemning to the flames those martyr men of God, whose names are this day fragrant in the churches of a land that was not known when Huss was burning. In the midst of a cabbage garden outside the gate, yet called the Huss Gate, we were led to the spot where he suffered; and returning, we called at the house in which he was lodged before he was brought to trial. But the streets of the city had grass growing in them; for of the forty thousand inhabitants who once filled these houses but seven thousand remain! Tenements are now tenantless that once were thronged with life. It was sad to wander by daylight through the streets without meeting a living being; and this was my experience here, and afterward in the island city of Rhodes. A chain stretched across the street sustained a lantern in the centre—a very convenient substitute for lamp-posts, if there are no carriages to pass, but a very awkward arrangement for a city infested with omnibuses.

Another day and the diligence brought us to Zurich, on the lake of the same name—the most thriving town in Switzerland. Here the lion-hearted reformer, Zwingle—the soldier of the cross, who perished on the field of battle—preached in the Cathedral, and dwelt in a house which is still standing and known as his. Here Lavater, the physiognomist, had a home and found a grave, over which the flowers are blooming. His was a lovely and loving spirit. Switzerland, strange to say, has not given birth to poets, but she is the mother of many noble sons, and her scenery has inspired the souls of the sons of song from other climes, who have wandered here and meditated among her lakes and hills.

Coming into Zurich, as we descended into the vale that holds the city and the lake, I had been charmed with the view; and now at the close of the next day, we were led to the height of one of the old ramparts, to behold a Swiss sunset, and certified to be " one of the finest scenes in Switzerland." The elevation, no longer needed for purposes of defence, has been tastefully transformed into a flower-garden. Enormous shade trees are crowning the summit, and on rude benches the romantically-disposed people, citizens and strangers, are seated. As we came to the top of the hill, the god of day was coming down from the midst of a dense cloud, like a mass of molten gold distilled into a transparent globe. His liquid face was trembling; but the world below sent back a smile of gladness as the king in his glory looked down upon it. The nearer summits seemed to catch the brightness first, and then in the distance others, invisible before, stood forth in their majesty, as if called into being by his quickening beams. At our feet was the lake, like a sea of glass. The spires of the city and the sloping hills were reflected from the mirror; and all over the country side, as far as the eye could reach, were thousands of white cottages and villas, the abode of wealth and peace and love—sweet Swiss homes, rejoicing in the sunshine as they send up their evening psalm of praise. It was a scene to make its impress on the memory, and to come up again and again in the far-off dreams of other lands and years.

To climb the Rigi, to spend the night on the top, to see the sun go down and get up in the morning, these are among the things to be done in a tour of Switzerland, and all these we set off to do, taking the steamer at Zurich and touching at Horgen, crossing over to Zug, and by steamer again to the little village of Arth, which lies at the foot of the hill we are to ascend. As we were approaching the shore, the reflection of the Rigi from the lake was so vivid and perfect that we could study the mountain in the water with as much satisfaction as a good-looking man contemplates his own person in a glass. Every particular cliff and crag, individual trees, and winding paths, and torrent beds, which we could see above, were defined with marvelous precision below. On landing, we dispatched a fleet mountain-boy ahead of us to engage beds at the house on the summit; for so many were with us on board the steamer, and so many more were doubtless climbing from the other side at the same time, that we were likely to have a bed on the floor unless we stole a march on our fellow-travellers. Most of them pushed upward from Arth, while we kept upon the plain for a mile or more to the village of Goldau, once the scene of a terrible catastrophe, the gloom of which still seems to be hanging over the ill-fated spot. The Rossberg Mountain is on the east of it, five thousand feet high, and in the year 1806 a mighty mass of it, some three miles long and a thousand feet thick, came sliding down into the valley, burying four hundred and fifty human beings in one untimely, dreadful grave. Travellers, like ourselves, who were making their way among these romantic regions, were suddenly overwhelmed in the deluge of earth and stones, and the places of their burial are unknown to this day. This event happened fifty years ago; but the broad, bare strip on the mountain side, which no verdure has since clad, is an ever-present record of the awful fall; and the great rocks that are lying on the opposite side of the valley, and away up the Rigi, are present witnesses of the messengers of death that came down in their wrath on that memorable day. The village church was then buried with the people who had been wont to frequent its courts, and nothing of it was ever found but the bell, which was carried a mile or more and now hangs in the steeple of another little temple filled with memorials of the ancient calamity.

Here we began the ascent of the Rigi. Some on horses, some on mules, more on foot, two or three ladies in sedan chairs, each borne by four stout men —a very lazy way of getting up 'hill, where health as well as pleasure is sought in travel; but every one choosing his own mode of ascent, and none having wings, we set off, as motley a party of mountain-climbers as ever undertook to scale a fortress. Four hours' steady travel, pausing only to look in occasion-ally at the chapels in which the Catholic pilgrims perform their prayers as they ascend to the church of " Mary in the Snow," which is about half-way up, brought us to the top where as yet the sun was half an hour high. And now, for the first time, did we know that we were in Switzerland. Not because we are on a very lofty mountain top—for the Rigi is not quite six thousand feet high—but we are on a mountain which stands so isolated that it affords us a better view than any other point, however elevated, of the mountains, the lakes, valleys, and villages, that make this land so peculiar for its beauty and grandeur. On the west, where we gazed with the deepest emotion as soon as we planted our feet on the summit, we saw the hoary Mount Pilatus, and at its base the Lake Lucerne, the most romantic of the Swiss lakes, and not exceeded by the scenery of any lake in the world. The city of Lucerne sends up its

towers and battlements, and the whole canton of that
name is spread out, with the River Reuss flowing
over its bosom. At our feet, nestling under the Rigi
and on the borders of the lake, is the village of
Kussnacht, and the chapel of William Tell, marking
the spot where the intrepid patriot pierced the
tyrant's heart with his unerring arrow. And now
the descending sun is pouring a flood of golden glory
over all this broad expanse of lake and forest, plain
and towering hills, whose peaks are touching the
blue skies, gilded with last rays of declining day.
Far southward we look away upon the mountains of
Unterwalden, of Berne, and of Uri, whose snow-clad
summits and blue glaciers are in full view, the
beautiful Jungfrau rising, queen-like, in the midst
of the magnificent group of sisters in white raiment.
The eastern horizon is supported by the snowy peaks
of the Sentis, the Glarnisch, and the Dodi; and the
two Mitres start up from the midst of that region
where Tell and his compatriots conspired to give
liberty to their native land. All around us are lakes,
so strangely nestled among the mountains that they
seem to be innumerable, peeping from behind the
hills and forests. And now the sound of the village
bells, and the Alpine horn, and the evening psalm,
comes stealing up the rugged sides of the Rigi, and
we are assured that, in this world of ice, and snow,

and eternal rocks, there are human hearts all warm and musical with the love of Him whose is the strength of the hills.

We had a short night's sleep, for what with a late supper and a crowd of people who had no beds, our rest was broken; and just as the dawn began, a monster, with a long wooden horn, marched through the halls, startling the sleepers with its blast, and forbidding sleep to come again. We had been warned over night that, at this signal, we must wrap up and run if we would see the sun rise; and as a posted notice in French forbade the use of the bed-blankets, we hurried on our clothes, and in a few moments stood, with a hundred others, like the Persian fire-worshippers, gazing eastward to catch the first glimpse of the coming king! Not long had we to wait. Another blast of the wooden trump gave notice of his approach, and presently a coal of fire seemed to be glowing in the crown of the mountain directly in front of us. It grew till the whole peak was ruddy with the glow, and then the great globe rose and rested on the summit! From this, as from a fount of light new-created and rejoicing in the first morning of its being, the streams of glory were poured out upon the world below and around us. Peak after peak, and long mountain ranges and ridges, domes and sky-piercing needles, and fields of fresh snow, and forests of living green,

began to smile in the sunlight. In the space of a
brief half hour the world was lighted up for the business of another day, and when we had had a cup of
wretched coffee and a bit of sour bread, we " marched
down again."

The steamer from Lucerne, on its daily trip from
that city, touches at Weggis, where we awaited its
coming, and were soon in the midst of the most
romantic scenery in Europe. From the water's edge
the mountains rise perpendicularly. Broken into
ridges, clothed with green forests or smooth pastures,
and now and then sheltering a hamlet in the openings,
the mountains stand around this lake with a majesty
too impressive for words. We have come into the
heart of a land of heroes. The waters of this lake are
like the life-blood of martyrs. This little village of
Gersau, on a sloping hillside, shut out from the rest
of the world by these mountain ramparts, was an
independent democracy of four hundred years, though
its domains were only three miles by two! Here, at
Brunnen, are painted, on the outer walls of a building
on the waterside, the effigies of the three great men
who, with William Tell, achieved the independence
of Switzerland in 1815. Across the lake, away up
among the ledges of the rocks, there lies a little plain,
an *oasis* in the wilderness, where, in the dead of night,
the three confederates met and laid their plans for the

deliverance of their country from the yoke of a foreign oppressor. **That spot is Grutli.** It is a holy place, for liberty was there **conceived,** and every patriot, from whatever land he comes, is thrilled when his eye looks on it. **Yet not** so sacred is Grutli as the land **upon** the opposite side of the lake, where the steamer slackens its **speed** as we are passing a little chapel that is built upon the margin of the lake. This chapel marks the spot where William Tell escaped **from** the boat in which he was a prisoner on his way to Gessler's prison at Kussnacht. It does savage violence to one's better feelings to be told that no such man as Tell was ever living in this land we are now exploring. He has been our ideal of a patriot chieftain from childhood, and we are not to be cheated out of him without a struggle. Skeptical critics may tell us, as they do, that Tell is a myth; but we have history for our faith to lean upon, and tradition tells us that this chapel was built in 1388, thirty-one years after the hero's death, and in presence of one hundred and fourteen persons who had known him when he was living. Such is our faith, and as we are passing by the chapel, to which, even unto this day, the Swiss make an annual pilgrimage **and have** a solemn mass performed within its narrow walls, and a sermon preached, we will tell the story of Tell.

When the year 1300 was coming in, Albert of Aus-

tria was ruling with a rod of iron over the dwellers in
these mountains. He sent magistrates among them
who exacted heavy taxes which they were unable to
pay, and imposed arbitrary and cruel punishments
upon them on slight occasions. Arnold, a peasant of
Uterwalden, was condemned for some insignificant
offence to give up a yoke of fine oxen, and the servant
of the bailiff seized them while Arnold was plowing
with them, and said, as he drove them off, " Peasants
may draw the plow themselves." Arnold smote the
servant, breaking two of his fingers, and fled. The
tyrant seized the father of Arnold and put out both
his eyes! Such cruelties became too many and too
grievous to be borne. Even the women — brave
souls !—refused to submit, and the wife of Werner
Stauffacher said to her husband : " Shall foreigners
be masters of this soil and of our property ? What
are the men of the mountain good for? Must we
mothers nurse beggars at our breasts, and bring up
our daughters to be maid-servants to foreign lords?
We must put an end to this!" Her husband was
roused, and went to Arnold, whose father's eyes had
been put out, and Walter Furst. These three held
their meetings for counsel at Grutli. Afterward each
of them brought ten men there, who bound themselves by a great oath to deliver their land from the
oppressor. This oath was taken in the night of No-

vember 17, 1307. Not long afterward the bailiff, Herman Gessler, when he saw the people more **restless and bold,** resol**ved to** humble them. He placed the ducal hat **of** Austria upon a pole, and ordered every one who passed by to bow down in reverence before it. William Tell, one of the men who had **taken the oath at** Grutli, held his head proudly erect as he passed, **and** when warned of the danger of such disobedience stoutly refused to bow. He was seized and **carried** before the bailiff, **who** was told **that Tell,** the most skillful archer of Uri, **had** refused **to pay** homage to the emblem of Austrian power. Enraged at Tell's audacity, Gessler exclaimed,

" Presumptuous archer, I will humble thee by the display of thine own skill. I will put an apple on the top of the head of thy little son ; shoot **it** off, and you shall be pardoned !"

In vain **did the** wretched father plead against such cruelty. **He could pierce the** eagle on the wing, and bring down the fleet chamois from the lofty rocks, but his arm would tremble and his eyesight fail him when he took aim at the head of his noble boy. **But** his remonstrances were **all in** vain. The **boy** was bound to a tree, and **the** apple set upon his head. The strong-hearted father took leave of his son, scarce hoping that he could spare him, and rather believing that his arrow would in another moment be rushing through his brain. With a prayer for help from Him who holds the stars in his hand, and without whose providence not a sparrow falls, the wretched father drew his bow. The unerring arrow pierced the apple, and the child was saved. Another arrow fell from underneath the garment of the archer as the shout of the people proclaimed the father's triumph.

"What means this?" demanded the tyrant.

"To pierce thy heart," replied Tell, "if the other had slain my son!"

Gessler ordered the man to be seized and bound, and hurried off to the dungeon he had built at Kussnacht. Fearing to trust the guards with their prisoner—for he knew not how far the spirit of rebellion might have spread—Gessler embarked in the boat with them, and hastened off lest the people should rise to the rescue of their countryman. The lake was subject then, as it is now, to sudden and fearful tempests. The wind rose and swept the waves over the boat, defying the skill of the boatmen, and threatening their speedy destruction. Tell was known for his skill with a boat as well as with a bow. Tyrants are always cowards, and when the tyrant saw that his own men were not able to manage the craft, he ordered Tell's bonds to be removed that he might take the helm in his hand. Steering the boat as near to the projecting rock of Axenberg as she could run, he suddenly leaped from it to the ledge, and the force of his leap sent the boat backward upon the lake. The prisoner was free. Pursuit was hopeless. He was at home among the **mountains**. Every path was familiar to him. But vengeance would be taken on those dearer than his own life. He resolved to preserve them by the death of the monster **who** had sought to make him slay his own son. With the speed of the chamois he sped his way across the mountains to the very place where he was to have been carried in chains, and there awaited the coming of Gessler. The tyrant came but to die. The arrow of the patriot drank his heart's blood. Then the inhabitants of the mountain fastnesses flew to arms. The minions of Austria were seized, and with a wonderful forbearance were not slain, but sent out of the country under an oath never to return. The King Albert came to subdue the rebels. On his way he was murdered by his nephew and a band of conspirators, whom he had thought his friends. He expired at the wayside, his head being supported by a peasant woman who found him lying in his blood. The children of the murdered man and his widow, and Agnes the Queen of Hungary, took terrible vengeance on the murderers, and, confounding the innocent with the guilty, shed blood like water. Agnes was a woman-fiend. As the blood of sixty-three guiltless knights was flowing at her feet, she said: "See, now I am bathing in May-dew!" One of the most distinguished of the enemies of the King, the Knight Rudolf, was, at her orders, broken on the rack, and while yet living was exposed to the birds of prey. While dying, he consoled his faithful wife, who alone knelt near him, and had in vain prostrated herself in the dust at the feet of Agnes, imploring her husband's pardon. But the war of oppression went on. An army marched into Switzerland, and to the many thousands of their invaders the men of Grutli could oppose only thirteen thousand. But they were all true men, and at Morgarten, on a rosy morning in 1315, they met the enemy and routed them utterly, after such deeds of valor as history scarcely elsewhere has recorded. This gave freedom to Switzerland. Of that struggle the first blow was struck by William Tell when he smote Gessler to the earth.

At the head of the Lake of Lucerne, and a few miles above the chapel of Tell, is the village of Fluelen, at which we rest only long enough to get away, for the low grounds, where the River Reuss comes down into the lake, breeds pestilence, and the inhabitants give proofs of the unhealthiness of the place by the number of cretins and goitred cases that are found among them. Two miles beyond is the old town of Altorf. Lapped in the midst of rugged mountains, which shut down closely on every side, it is secluded from the world that is familiar with its name. Here, on this village green, in front of the old tower, a fountain, surmounted by a statue, marks the spot where William Tell shot the apple from the head of his son. The tree on which the **ducal hat was** hung by Gessler, and the same to which the boy was bound, is said to have remained **there** three hundred years after the event. The *tower* **dates** back **of that time, as records still** in existence prove it to be more than five **hundred and** fifty years old. To this day the hunters **of** Uri come down to Altorf to try their skill with the rifle, which has now taken the place of the bow and arrow.

A few miles further on **we** came **to the River Reuss, in** which William Tell **was drowned** while **attempting to save the life of a boy.** There was **something** sublime **in the** thought that **a man** whose **name is now** identified with the patriots and heroes of the world should finally lose his life in the performance of **a deed** that requires more **of the self-**sacrificing spirit than to **scale the walls of a** fortress **and** perish in the midst of a nation's praise.

The men of this **region are spoken of** as the finest race in Switzerland. **We** had no reason to think them remarkable ; but the women, who were making **hay in** the meadows while the men **were** off hunting, were certainly very good-looking for women who work in the fields in all weathers, braving the storms of rain and snow, tending the sheep and cattle on the hillsides, and carrying the hay on their backs to the barns.

As we pressed our way up the great Saint Gothard road, frowning precipices rise a thousand feet high, black, jagged rocks, almost bare of vegetation, shutting out the sunlight, and making a solitude fearful and solemn, its silence rarely disturbed but by the passing traveller and the ceaseless dashing of the river, which, instead of flowing, tumbles from ledge to ledge. In the spring of the year the avalanches make the passage still more fearful.

Twenty or thirty thousand persons travel over this pass every year; and to keep the current in this direction, the cantons of Uri and Tessin built this splendid carriage-path, as smooth as a floor, and so firm in its substructures as to resist the violence of the storms and the swollen torrents that so often rush frightfully down these gorges. Twice was the work swept away before this road was completed, which, it is believed, will stand while the mountains stand. So rapid is the ascent, that the road often doubles upon itself, and we are going half the time backward on our route. Sometimes the road is hewn out of the solid rock in the side of the precipice, which

hangs over it as a roof, and again it is carried over
the roaring stream that is boiling in a gulf four
hundred feet below. Toiling up the gorge, with the
savage wildness of the scenery becoming every
moment more savage still, we reach the Devil's
Bridge. More than five hundred years ago, an old
abbot of Einsiedeln built a bridge over an awful
chasm here ; but such is the fury of the descending
stream, the whole mass of waters being beaten into
foam among the rocks that lift their heads through
the cataracts—such is the horrid ruggedness of the
surrounding scenery, and so unlikely does it appear
that human power could ever have reared a bridge
over such a fearful chasm, it has been called, from
time immemorial, the Devil's Bridge. A Christian
traveller would much prefer to ascribe its origin to a
better source ; for whatever miracle it required, we
might refer it to the skill and goodness of Him who
hung the earth upon nothing, and holds the stars in
his hand. We were quite cold when we reached the
bridge, and, quitting the carriage, walked over it to
study its structure, and enjoy the grandeur of a scene
that has hardly an equal even in this land of the
sublime and terrible. At this spot the River Reuss
makes a tremendous plunge at the very moment
that it bends nearly in a semicircle, and a world of
rocks has been hurled and heaped in the midst of the

torrent, to increase the rage and roar of the waters, arrested for a moment only to gather strength for a more terrific rush into the abysses below. We approach the parapet, and look calmly over, and there, far below us, is another bridge, which, becoming useless by age and the violence of the elements, was superseded by this new and costly structure.

We crossed the bridge and soon entered the long *Gallery of Uri*—a tunnel cut through the solid rock —a hard but the only passage, as the torrent usurps the whole of the gorge, and the precipice above admits no possible path overhead. A hundred and fifty years ago this hole was bored, and before that time the only passage was made on a shelf supported by chains let down from above, on which a single traveller could creep, if he had the nerve, in the midst of the roar and the spray of the torrent in the yawning gulf below him. To add to the gloom and terror of the scene about us, a storm, with thunder and lightning broke upon us as we emerged from this den, and right speedily set in while as yet we had no shelter. We had come into an upper valley, a vale five thousand feet above the level of the sea, where no corn grows, though the land flows with milk and honey. The cows and goats find pasture at the foot of the glaciers, and the bees, who find flowers even in these realms of eternal snow, make their nests in

the stunted trees and the holes in the rocks. At Andermatt, a village among the mountains, we come
upon an inn whose many lighted windows invited us
to seek refuge from the increasing storm, and we
entered a room already thronged with travellers who
had reached it before us, many of them coming down,
and they were now rejoicing over a smoking supper.
They made us welcome, and in the good cheer we
soon forgot the fatigues and the perils of the most exciting and exhausting day we had had in Switzerland.

"Blessed be he who first invented sleep," the
weary traveller says, with Sancho, whenever night
comes, and wherever, if he is so happy as to have a
place wherein and on to lay his head. Sleep, that
will not come for wooing to him who wastes his hours
in idleness at home, now folds her soft arms lovingly
about him, kisses his eyelids, whispers gentle memories in his soul, and dreams of the loved and the distant are his as the swift night-hours steal away. The
nights are not long enough; for when the first nap is
past the sun of another day is struggling to get over
the hill-top and look down into the vale of Andermatt!

We might pursue this St. Gothard highway over
into Italy, but we have not yet seen Switzerland.—
Hitherto we have been traversing only the great

roads of travel. Now we will strike off into the regions where wheel carriages have never yet been
seen. The Furca Pass leads off from the St. Gothard
road, and with a guide to pilot us, we struck into a
narrow defile. Away above us the blue glacier of
St. Anne was shining in the morning sun, and now
we are at the foot of a beautiful waterfall that leaps
from its bosom into the vale below. Here are the
remains of an awful avalanche of rocks and earth that
came down a few years since, on a little hamlet clustering on the hillside. The inhabitants fled as they
heard it coming, but a maiden, tending a babe, refused to leave her precious charge, and could not fly
with it as rapidly as the rest. · She perished with it in
her arms. Soon we came to a mountain stream which
crossed our path, and the bridge had been swept
away by an avalanche only the very night before.
There were no signs of danger now, and we could
scarcely believe the stories that were told us of the
sudden destruction wrought by these thunderbolts of
snow, and ice, and earth, which are the terror of
these regions. The village we slept in last night is
protected by a forest of trees so arranged as to receive
and ward off the slides ; but they come at times with
such force as to cut off the trees, and bury everything
in undistinguished ruin.

This *pedestrianism* is very well to boast of at home,

and for those who are used to it and fond of it, it
may be a very agreeable mode of travel; I confess I
was tired of it the first day, and took to the horse as
decidedly a better, as it certainly is an easier method
of transit. It was just about as much as I could do to
walk, and think of the number of miles we had gone,
and had yet to go, with scarcely any spirit to enjoy the
romance of the scenery, the glaciers and waterfalls,
the precipices and snowy summits that were around
me; and groaning all the while with the burden of
locomotion. It was another thing altogther to sit
on a horse, and folding one's arms, to look upward
and around rejoicing in the wonders of God's world,
and breathing in with the mountain air, the rich in-
spirations of the scene.

We are now so far up in the world that the snow,
though the month of August is closing, is lying by
the side of the pathway, while the wild flowers, in
bright and beautiful colors, are blooming in the sun,
and close to the edges of these chilling banks. On
our right hand the Galenstoch glacier lies among the
peaks of naked rock that, like the battlements of
some thunder-riven castle, shoot upward eleven thousand feet into the clear blue sky. We are among the
ice-palaces of the earth. I hug my great coat closely,
as the cold winds from these eternal icebergs search
me, and in a few minutes reached the inn at the sum-

mit of the Furca Pass. Snow-clad summits of distant mountains glistened in the noonday sun, and
blue glaciers wound along and down the gorges, and
so far above the valleys were we now that it seemed
like a world without inhabitants, desolate, cold, and
majestic, in its solitude and icy splendor.

The descent was too rapid for safe riding, and, giving the horse to the guide, who would lead him
around, I leaped down the steep declivity, and soon
found myself in a lovely vale. Turning suddenly
around a promontory, a scene of such grandeur and
beauty burst upon our sight as we had not yet encountered, even in this land of wonders. An ocean lashed
into ridges and covered with foam, then suddenly
congealed, would not be the spectacle! Freeze the
cataract of Niagara and the rapids above it, and let
them rise a thousand feet into the air; congeal the
clouds of spray, the falling jewelry; pile up pyramids
and minarets, and columns, and battlements of ice,
and then, at each side of this magnificent scene, set
a tall mountain, with green pasturage on its sides,
and its head crowned with everlasting snow, and you
have some faint image of the Glacier of the Rhone!
Travellers have called it the Frozen Ocean of Switzerland. But it is more than this. And yet out of
its bosom, its cold but melting heart, the River Rhone
is flowing. This is its source. The daring adven-

turer may follow it up, beneath the blue arches and between the polished walls, till he finds himself far away in these caverns of ice, where no living thing abides. And here he learns the great design of a benificent Creator in forming these glaciers. The snows of winter are here stored up, and, instead of being suddenly melted in the spring, and then sent down in torrents to devastate the lands through which the overwhelming currents would be borne, they are melted by degrees, and led by channels through these mountain passes into the river beds that water all the countries of Europe! For this great purpose Switzerland was built! It has been lightly said that this Swiss country looks as if it had been the leavings of the world when creation was finished, and the refuse material that could not be conveniently worked in had been thrown in dire confusion, heaps on heaps, into this wilderness of jagged rocks, and shapeless mountains, and disordered ranges of hill and vale—impracticable for man or beast—a rude, wild land, doomed to perpetual poverty, and existing only to be an object of curiosity to the traveller. But we find it to be the great fountain of living waters, pouring its inexhaustible streams into the wide and many lands below, carrying fertility and beauty over millions of acres, and food and gladness to countless homes.

A hard hill to climb was the Grimsel. Sometimes I rode, but more frequently I was content to toil upward on my own feet, without taxing the jaded horse with my weight to be added to his own. But when we reached the summit, and overtook other parties who were before us, and were overtaken by yet others coming up behind, we formed a picturesque procession of some forty or fifty pilgrims, who wound slowly along the banks of the *Dead Sea*—a lake that lies away up among these frozen heights, and derives its name from the fact that it was once the grave of a multitude of soldiers who perished in the fight in these mountain fastnesses.

The vale of the Grimsel is beneath us, and just before the sun sets we reach the Hospice, and eagerly ask for lodgings. On the borders of a little lake, in the bottom of a narrow valley, surrounded by almost perpendicular rocks, stands this solitary house, in former years inhabited by friendly monks who made it their pious care to entertain the traveller and furnish free hospitality to the poor. Now it is a hotel, and a very poor one at that, where you may get a supper, and a bed, and a large bill in the morning. This is a dreary spot now, and in the winter more fearful it must be.

In the morning we found the path that led us out of the valley to the Glaciers of the Aar. The moun-

11

tain of earth, rocks, ice and snow that we encountered put to flight all ideas we had formed of a glacier. We seemed to have come to a vast heap of sand, or to the *debris* brought down by an avalanche, but from the base of it a torrent was rushing of a dirty milky hue, and out of its front we could see rocks of blue ice projecting. Now and then a mass of earth or a huge boulder would be hurled along down the precipice.

And this mighty mass of ice, decaying at the front and pressed down from above, is slowly moving onward at the rate of some twelve inches a day. If a stream of water running across it cuts a wide seam, so that the mass is suddenly brought down, the shock will throw up the ice in ridges, and in various fantastic shapes, as if some great explosion had upheaved the frozen ocean, and the fragments had come down in wild confusion, like the ruins of a crystal city. Then the sun gradually melts the towers, and they assume shapes of dazzling beauty, palaces of glass, silver domes, and shining battlements—making us to wonder that so much beauty and magnificence are seemingly wasted in these dreary solitudes.

Nestled charmingly among the hills is the sweet village of Interlaken. The plain which it adorns stretches from Lake Thun to Lake Brienz, and the quiet retreat it furnishes is improved by hundreds of English people, who make it a summer residence. It combines two advantages, very rarely blended in this world— it is *cheap* and *genteel*. A large number of neat boarding-houses, some of them aspiring to the rank of first-class hotels, are scattered along the main street of the village ; and at the *Hotel des Alpen*, the largest establishment and admirably kept, the traveller may find good rooms and board for a dollar a day, and at even less than that if he is disposed to be very economical. We had crossed the Wengern Alp and passed the vale of Grindewald ; had seen an avalanche come down from the side of the Jungfrau, and been amused with the little cascade called the Staubach, about which poets and printers have gone into ecstasies ; and we were glad to find so quiet, beautiful, and civilized a spot in which to sit down for a few days and rest.

While we were at Interlaken we made a beautiful excursion on Lake Brienz to the Giesbach Fall. It has some peculiarities that claim for it the very first rank among the falls of Switzerland. See the little stream that issues as from a cleft in the rock, nearly a thousand feet above the waters of the lake. Then among the dark evergreens the white flood comes swelling and plunging into secret abysses where the eye can not search its hidings, but it rises again with a widened torrent, and now spreads a broad bosom of waters over a mighty precipice ; and here a bridge has been thrown across in front of the falls, and a gallery cut away behind it, so that it may be circumvented by the visitor who is provided with an overcoat of India rubber, or is willing to take a thorough sponging for sake of the submarine excursion. When I had completed the circuit, a lady was regretting that she could not venture on the tour, but her scruples were instantly removed when I offered her my water-proof, and in a few minutes she returned "charmed" with her trip. Once more the swollen mass of waters plunges over the rocks and shoots out into the lake, in one of the most romantic and beautiful regions that is to be found in this wildly beautiful land.

I pass over the experiences of a few days' travel, and come suddenly to the summit of the Col de Balm.

Mont Blanc is in sight ! Not a faint and doubtful view of a peak among a hundred peaks, but the monarch of the Alps stands there—a king in his glory, revealed from his summit to the base. A cloud is gathered like a halo on his head ; but it rises and vanishes as we look upon it with silent admiration and awe. Around him are the Aiguilles or Needles, bare pinnacles of rock stretching up like guards into the heavens, and between are the glaciers—reflecting now the rays of the noonday sun, and among them

UNDER THE GEISBACH FALLS.

the *Mer de Glace*—winding along down the gorges, and resting their cold feet in the vale below.

Afterward I saw Mont Blanc from its base, and sought other heights from which it might be surveyed, but I could find nothing comparable to the view from the *Col de Balm*. There it stands, towering fifteen thousand eight hundred and ten feet toward the sky, the loftiest summit in Europe, with thirty-four glaciers around it ; and as I gazed, it was a strange question to discuss—but one that might well be argued till sundown—is old Ocean, or Niagara, a sublimer sight ?

It seems so near the sky that the blue firmament kisses its brow. It is so far off, yet so near, so bright and pure, that the angels might be sporting on its summit and be safe from the intrusion of men. It is a *solemn* mountain. Even the hills of Syria and Palestine, on which I afterward gazed, Lebanon and Hermon, Carmel and Horeb, with their hallowed memories clustering on them, were not more impressive than this hoary hill—forever clothed in white raiment, standing there like an ivory throne for the King of Kings !

We went down into the vale of Chamouni, and at evening saw the stars like diamonds sparkling in the crown of the monarch, and then the moonbeams fell all cold upon his crest. We rose the next morning early, and saw the summit of Mont Blanc in a blaze of glory long before the dwellers in the vale had seen the rays of the rising sun.

And then we left Switzerland.

CHAPTER XIV.

SAXON SWYTZ.

A model guide—The Bastei—Banditti of old—A cataract to order—Scaling a Rampart—Konigstein—the Kuhstall—the Great Winterberg—Prebisch Thor—Looking Back.

I N a corner of Saxony is a miniature Switzerland. They call it Saxon Switzerland; perhaps the name is not well chosen, for it has one feature only of Swiss scenery—exceeding beauty. Only three days are required to see it, and two will give a good traveller all the more prominent points, in a series of views, the romantic loveliness of which will linger a lifetime in the memory of one who has seen them. The Elbe is now navigated by little steamboats, which English enterprise introduced, but a better. way to reach

(247)

Saxon Swytz, if you are pressed for time, **is** to go with us by rail to Rathen, and there strike off into the mountains. A local guide must be had at once, before you take a step. It was now the height of the travelling season, and on a fine morning in July **we** found ourselves at a small tavern on the banks of the Elbe, with half a dozen men about us pressing their **claims to** be employed as guides among the mountains. "**Do you** speak English?" we inquired of one: **to which he answered " Yes," and** this **with** the frequent exclamation "look here" proved to be the Alpha and Omega of our German's knowledge of English. He had a book of certificates which former travellers had given him, and as they were sure **he** could not read one of them, they had **very** freely commended him as ignorant, stupid, temperate and faithful, acquainted with **the** country, **and** probably no worse a guide **than the rest. He was** our man. We could get out of him all **that** was necessary, and as he pleaded hard for employment, and knew three words of English more than the rest, we took **him,** and in five minutes he **took** us into a small **boat to** pull us over the Elbe. Instantly **the** bewitching scenery began **to surround us. The** river was here so winding that we could see a little way only, either up or down, but the lofty banks rose so abruptly from the water and the rocks, in the midst of which evergreens were growing, hung so fearfuly above us, that we seemed to be suddenly borne into a land of enchantment. We landed on the other side, a " house of refreshment," where German ladies and gentlemen were recruiting themselves with beer, which like an overflowing stream appears to come from some exhaustless fountain. Now we are to decide between a pedestrian tour and mules. We were not long in making up our minds, and soon we were off on the beasts; sorry beasts they were; better men than Balaam might have wished for a sword, or some more fitting weapon to make them go. They were indifferent to all minor arguments, such as words and kicks, and only conscious of the *a posteriori* mode of reasoning, to which the muleteer in the rear continually resorted. We left the common road, and by a narrow path commenced the ascent to one of the most celebrated and splendid points of observation, the Bastei. On either side of us as we are ascending, huge precipices frown and deep grottoes in which the fairy spirits of these forests may be supposed to dwell, invite us to rest as weary of the upward way. Now a waterfall, beautiful as water in motion always is, and picturesque as a cascade in the green woods must be, tempts us to linger and take the spray on our heated brows. Through dense shades of evergreen forests, by a path so steep, at

11*

times, that it is difficult to keep your seat in the saddle, we toil on, and in the course of an hour have triumphed over the hardships of the hill, and have reached the summit of the loftiest bastion in the world. It is as perpendicular as a wall that has been reared for defence. The rock on which we were standing projects from the front of the precipice, and we are hanging six hundred feet above the Elbe. The river winds round the base of the mountain, and both up and down the stream for many miles the eye rests on similar heights on the same side that we are standing. Behind us, Ossa upon Pelion seems to be piled. Giant rocks stand up there in solemn and solitary grandeur, as if by some great convulsion of nature the earth had been torn from their sides, and they were left to brave earthquakes and thunderbolts with their naked heads and sides exposed to perpetual storms. Yet the bravery of man has bridged the horrid chasms that yawn between these separated cliffs, and they have in times past, been the hiding places of banditti, who from these heights could watch the Elbe, and make their descent upon the hapless navigator of the peaceful stream. On one of the rocks is a huge boulder so evenly balanced on the very pinnacle that it has been called "Napoleon's Crown," and another from a fancied resemblance, " the Turk's head," and all of them have titles more or less fitting. Across the river, and in front of us, the plain spreads wide and rises as it recedes from the shore till it meets a range of wooded mountains. From the midst of this plain there rise immense cones, suddenly and remarkably, strange formations, a study for the geologist, probably left there when all the surrounding masses were worn away by the Elbe in making its way through this mountainous region. The country is full of legends connected with each and all of these strange columns, the summits of which are sometimes crowned with castles, and one of them, the Lilienstein, is so perpendicular and lofty, that the Elector of Saxony and King of Poland, when he had scaled its heights, left a record of his memorable exploit. In the hiding places of this wild and rugged rock, the spirits of the woods are supposed to hover over concealed treasures. " A holy nun miraculously transported from the irregularities of her convent to the summit of the Normenstein, that she might spend her days in prayer and purity in its caverns, is commemorated in the name of the rock, and the ' *Jungfernsprung*,' or leap of the Virgin, perpetuates the memory of the Saxon maid who when pursued by a brutal lustling threw herself from the brink of its hideous precipice to die unpolluted."—RUSSELL.

Konigstein, nearly a thousand feet high, with its

impregnable fortress, we shall attempt this afternoon, and enter it with a flag of truce, as it was never taken by force. We came up here for the sake of view, and fully repaid for the toil of the ride, we are now prepared to descend by another route, when we are told for the first time that the mules are not for us to ride down, we must foot it, and the mules be driven by the same road they came up. Through the wildest of all wild gorges our winding way led us, at the base of jagged rocks of fearful height, out of the broken breasts of which huge trees were growing, threatening to fall, yet clinging for life to the crevices in which their roots were fastened. Now and then a scared eagle would scream and soar away from his nest, but rarely did a sound except the murmur of water, and the sighing of the air through the narrow defile disturb the deep stillness of that solitude. That projecting rock, with its adjacent pillars of stone, is called the Devil's Pulpit, and that, the Throne, and so other points of peculiar configuration have names more or less fanciful, which a lively imagination has given them. Suddenly, we came upon a family of peasants, who have a hut under the shelter of the rocks, and a few articles of refreshment for weary travellers; sweet milk, and bread and cheese, and a bottle or two of liquor—but they are chiefly and decidedly in the cold water line; they are in the cataract business!

The little stream that takes this gorge in its way to the Elbe, at this point would make a leap of some twenty feet among the rocks. With an economy that would do honor to American foresight, these people have made a dam across the rivulet before it falls, and thus accumulating the waters, have them ready for a grand splurge, when a party come along who are willing to pay a few pence for the pleasure of seeing the performance. One of our people gave the word of command in German, of which a free translation would be " Let her slide," and down came the young Niagara. But for the ludicrous idea of an artificial cataract in the mountains, the sight would have been very pretty. The gorge hitherto had been so narrow and deep, that the sun never shines to the bottom, and no flowers ever cheer its gloom ; but now the sun lighted up the falling drops, making them like great diamonds, as we from behind the sheet looked out upon the extempore waterfall. It was a walk of four or five miles, through such scenes, to the place from which we had started, and here we awaited the coming of a little steamer which was creeping along the banks to pick up passengers. It picked us up, and dropped us in a few minutes at Konigstein, or the *King's Stone*. The little town with a thousand people in it, would not deserve a call, but it is in our way to the fortress on the summit of the rocky height behind. The road is paved all the way with large square stones, making a carriage path, up which enormous guns are dragged for its defence. To this day it boasts of never having fallen into the hands of the enemy. Napoleon, with incredible toil, carried some of his heaviest pieces of ordnance to the top of *Lilienstein*, but could not reach it with his balls. Much of the distance up which we toiled, the road is cut through a living rock, which rises a solid wall on either side, and winds around the hill, till we come to a wooden bridge over an awful chasm, which separates the passage from the cliff on which the fortress stands, on a platform two miles in circuit, inaccessible except to friends, or to foes with wings. One portcullis passed, and we have only come to the gate. Iron spikes projecting from the stonework threaten us as we approach. At the gate, soldiers are looking through the port-holes, and challenge us to stand. They take our cards and passports to the commander, and soon return with permission for us to enter. But once admitted within the massive gate, we have still a long bridge across the moat to pass, and then by a covered passage at an angle of forty-five degrees, over a stone road, up which cannon are drawn by a windlass, we come out on the summit of the hill to a scene of transcendent beauty, and of the richest historic interest. The ground is neatly laid out in walks and

gardens; there are fields of pasture for herds of cattle
and of grain raised for the support of the garrison.
Their unfailing supply of water is drawn from a well
eighteen hundred feet deep! We held a mirror to the
sun, and sent the reflected light away down into that
mysterious depth, and watched it sporting on the
waters. Then we poured a glass of water into the
well, and in *thirty seconds* by the watch, the sound
returned to our listening ears. Sound travels eleven
hundred and forty-two feet in a second, and would
therefore be less than two seconds in coming up; so
that if our measure of time was correct, it must have
taken the water nearly half a minute to travel down to
the surface from which it had been drawn. We drank
of that well and found the water cool and delightful.
Standing on the ramparts, which are defended by
enormous guns, we overlooked the plains on one hand,
the river and the romantic hills of Saxon Switzerland
on the other. Again the columnal rocks arrested our
attention, more peculiar now that we are nearer. Far,
very far higher than the loftiest cathedral spire, and
not broader at the base, they rise in solitary grandeur,
where the Great Architect of the earth first placed
them, and where they will stand till all the cathedrals
and fortresses and pyramids of man's building have
crumbled into dust.

We bought a few pieces of Bohemian glass ware

as souvenirs of this visit, and then reluctantly turning away from the scene, which seemed more beautiful the longer we dwelt upon it—so it is with beauty ever—we reluctantly came down.

A German full of humor, a rare sort of German, for they are not addicted to the humorous at home or abroad, had joined us in our pedestrian tour to Konigstein; and having just come down the river as we were going up, he gave us the information we asked for of the upper country. He spoke a "leetel English," and that made his answers more amusing.

"Which is the best hotel for us in Ichandau?" we inquired.

"They is dree hotels, one is so bad as de toder," said he.

"And what shall we find at Winterberg?"

"Noding but gray sand-stone and sheating strangers."

With this very unpromising prospect, we waited for the steamer to come along to take us to Ichandau and Winterberg.

Steaming on the Elbe is a very small affair; a narrow boat with a long nose, moves on at the rate of four or five miles an hour, and stops at the end of a plank or two put out from the shore for a wharf. One of these filled with pleasure travellers in the aft

and the long bows covered with peasantry, touched
at Konigstein, and received us. It was near sunset.
We were often in the deep shadows of the mountains,
and then through the openings, or as the circuitous
river brought us into the day again, the declining
sun streamed upon us with exceeding beauty. Tired
with the hard day's work, having mounted the Bastei
on one side of the Elbe, and Konigstein on the other,
I was glad to lie off upon a bench and enjoy the
luxury of this cool delicious hour. Ichandau
charmingly dropped down among the mountains, is
an old town, but only remarkable as the point from
which to set off on exploring expeditions into the
interior of Saxon Switzerland. The three hotels
were filled with company, who were spending their
evening in eating and drinking at small tables on
the piazzas, or under the shade trees, a practice of
which the Germans are more fond than any other
people I have met. We found beds in a great ball-
room, with low partitions running between them, so
that when the room was needed for dancing, these
could be readily removed. I was in want of some
refreshments after the fatigues of the day, and when
the various drinks that I called for were not to be had,
the waiter asked me if I would have " Yahmah Kah
rhoom," which I declined after finding that he meant
Jamaica rum. Without any night-cap of the sort,

and spite of more noise than would have been agreeable if we had not been so weary, we had a good night of it, and rose with the sun to continue our pilgrimage. A carriage was ready for us, to convey us six miles from Ichandau, through a romantic glen, wide enough to afford beautiful meadows on both sides of a stream, by the side of which a good road was leading us into the mountains. The women were at work making hay, scores of them, and not a man to be seen. The brightest of Cole's landscapes among the Kaatskill mountains came to my mind as we rode on, and admired the green hill sides; then, as we advanced, gnarled trees stood out upon the rocks, immense piles, jagged, riven, blasted and heaped one upon another in such orderly confusion, that it seemed as if architecture had done its worst to make towers for giants here.

Our ride terminated at *Peishll Swarl*, where we were surrounded by a troop of men who had horses to let, and in their German tongue, they clamored most importunately for us to engage them. Our friend, the Rev. Dr. K., being of German origin, and better skilled in the language than the rest of us, we left to make the bargain, while we selected the best horses for ourselves with that beautiful selfishness so common to the human species. As we deserved, and as he deserved, we got the worst of the lot, and he was soon mounted on a handsome pony, that easily led the party, the whole day. Now it may be known to some who read this, that Dr. K. is not a very tall divine, but what he lacks of being gigantic in height, he makes up in breadth, so that seated upon this little animal about four feet high, and riding up a steep mountain pass, when seen from before, he looked like a horse with a man's head, but when we gazed upward at him from behind, we saw a man with a horse's tail. I had selected a good looking beast, but it had a lady's saddle to which I objected, as it was "Fur damen," for women : but the owner promptly met the objection by pulling away the *rest*, and crying out with a laugh "Fur herren," for men. Immediately on mounting we struck into the woods, and soon into a narrow pass where the rocks had been cleft asunder just far enough for a path for a single horseman; a hundred steps lead up to the summit of a lofty hill whence a fine view is had of the columnal rocks and numerous peaks of mountains, whose hard names would not be remembered if we were to repeat them. On this height is the famous *Kuhstall*, or in English *Cow-stall*, a cave in the rock, to which in the Thirty Years' war, the peasants in the plains below were in the habit of driving their cattle for safety, and in these all but inaccessible solitudes, the Protestant Christians fled from persecution, and hid themselves as their primitive brethren did, in dens and caves of the earth. One of these recesses, more retired and better sheltered than the rest, had the name of the " Woman's bed." Who can tell the sufferings, who can tell the joys that the people of God have known in these high places ? No cathedral service could be more sublime than prayer and praise on the mountain tops, and in the grottoes of these rocky heights, where now the weary traveller from a land on the other side of the sea, sits down and recalls the story of those times that " tried men's souls." Through a narrow fissure in the rock we ascended to a platform that makes the roof of the Kuhstall. Before us was a valley surrounded by mighty rocks and pine-covered hills, an amphitheatre in which the present population of the earth could stand, and it required but little stretch of the imagination to believe that a strong voice could be heard by the multitude so assembled. My servant led my horse to the edge of the precipice, many hundred feet high, and he planted his feet firmly on the edge, as if he were accustomed to the spot, and there stood for me to enjoy the glorious scene. On this lofty and far away height, some women had a stand for the sale of strawberries and cream, the taste of which did not interfere with the beauties of the prospect, as I sat on my horse eating, and **gazing,** and making these notes. But we cannot be on the mount always. **We** crossed the valley, **and on** the **narrow road** met parties of German **travellers smoking as they trudged** along, women **and some children, making the tour** of the mountains **on foot, and in the course of a** couple of hours we commenced the ascent of the Great Winterberg, and **climbed it to the summit.**

Here at the height of **one** thousand **seven** hundred feet above the sea we found a good hotel, with every comfort for the entertainment of travellers **and a** fine lookout from **which may be had the grandest** sight in Saxon Switzerland. I wrote the names of sixteen **noble** peaks **that stood up around me, with** their thick green foliage, **the** intervening **valleys** dense with forest, the beautiful Elbe **silently** circling **the base** of the mountains, and **the pillars of** stone rising like sentinels away **off in the plains beyond.** **Our** way lay through the **thick** forest, as **we came** down to the *Prebisch Thor* or Gate, a mighty arch, **a** hundred **feet broad, and sixty-five feet high, a** wonderful freak **of nature, not so lofty as the Natural** Bridge of Virginia, but more impressive from **the** position it occupies, **away up in these** mountains, more than a thousand feet above **the river.** It might be the **gate** of the **world!** How mean **the splendid** arches of Conquerors, compared with this which the

King of Kings had reared. I exclaimed with reverence as I saw it, " Lift up your heads, O ye gates,
and be ye lifted up ye everlasting doors, and the
King of glory shall come in." A score of visitors
were here before us. A row of romantic cottages,
clinging like eagles' nests, to the ledges of the rocks,
furnish rest and refreshment to the pilgrims, and we
sat down in sight of this stupendous wonder of
nature, and dined, while we sought to take in at the
same time, an image of it which we should never
lose. Underneath the arch ambitious travellers have
vied with each other in seeing how high they could
inscribe their names, and some have made the
records so as to resemble tombstones, rows of which
are cut into the solid rock. Visitors from many different lands, have in their several languages left their
impressions in the book which is kept here for the
purpose, and we added our names and a faint
transcript of our feelings to the records of the
Prebisch Thor. The descent was by several hundred
steps, sometimes of wood, then of stone, and again
of earth, which we made on foot, while the horses
were led by a longer road around. As we came
down into the valley, we met—for we were now in
Bohemia, under Austrian rule—numerous beggars
with various claims upon our charity. Among them
was an old woman who stretched out a pair of naked

arms dried to the bone and the color of bronze, her
feet and the lower part of her legs, her head and
breast were bare, and all so dried and dark, so unlike
a woman that it made me sick to look at her. "Can
a woman come to that?" I asked myself, as I gave my
servant some money for the old crone, and hurried
on for fear she would get before me again to thank
me. In the stream which comes leaping down from
the mountain, were women and children wading,
with hooks in their hands to catch the floating bits
of wood, and bring them ashore for fuel. The narrow
defile through which we passed was picturesque, and
the great mountains behind us often called us back
to look at the heights where we had stood, and so
now looking back, and now plunging on and down,
into the regions of human dwellings, by little mills
on the leaping stream, and by the side of cottages
where some taste appeared in vines and flowers, we
arrived at *Hirniskretchen*, on the Elbe. Here we
crossed the river, and by the railroad which comes
along on the other side, we reached in a few moments
the station at *Bodenbach* the frontier town of
Austria. The train is detained an hour, while the
passports, and luggage of all the passengers are
examined with that minuteness which is always suffered in small towns more inconveniently than in
cities. Some of the ladies' trunks made such revela-

tions of articles of dress and jewelry, that no protestations of their being designed only for personal use were of any avail. It was impossible in the eyes of these simple officers, that women could need so many gloves, and laces and bracelets, and they were all examined even to the smallest boxes of "*bijouterie*" which could be found. We had no difficulty whatever, being very slightly loaded with baggage of any sort, especially of that sort which custom houses, those pests of nations, are so apt to challenge. At last we were pronounced all right, and the train set off, through a beautiful country, a massive church standing on one side of the river, a towering castle on the other; now rushing by Aussig, a precipice and gorge of frightful height, where the road hugs the rock into the side of which it is cut, and so through numerous pleasing villages, we are hurried on to the ancient city of PRAGUE.

Sheldon and Company.

A Select List

OF

PUBLICATIONS.

—◆◆◆—

Messrs. SHELDON & COMPANY beg leave to say that their publications can generally be found at all Book Stores, News Depots, and Religious Depositories. When not obtainable at these places, any book on the list will be forwarded, prepaid by mail, on receipt of the retail prices annexed to each book.

Special attention is called to the list of School and College Text Books. Samples of these are sent to Teachers and Educators by mail prepaid, on receipt of one half the prices annexed.

NEW YORK:

SHELDON & COMPANY, 115 NASSAU ST.,

Publishers and Booksellers.

1860.

J. P. Thompson, D.D

The Christian Graces. 16mo., ... 75
Memoir of the Rev. D. T. Stoddard. 12mo., . 1 00

S. Irenæus Prime, D.D.

The Bible in the Levant. 16mo., . . . 75

William J. Hoge, D.D.

Blind Bartimeus. 16mo., ... 75

Rev. W. P. Balfern.

Glimpses of Jesus. 16mo., . . . 60
Lessons from Jesus. 16mo., ... 75

Rev. Henry M. Field.

From Copenhagen to Venice. 12mo., . . 1 00

Rev. Alfred S. Patton.

Losing and Taking of Mansoul. 12mo., . . 1 00

Mrs. Maria T. Richards.

Life in Israel. 12mo., . . . 1 00

Manton Eastburn, D.D.

Thornton's Family Prayers. 12mo., . . . 75
"   "   "   Fine ed., red edges, . 1 00

John Dowling, D.D.

The Power of Illustration. 18mo., . . 30
The Judson Memorial. 16mo., . . 60

Hermann Olshausen, D.D.

Commentaries on the New Testament. 6 vols.,
8vo. Ed. A. C. Kendrick, D.D., . . . 12 00

The same. 8vo., sheep, ... 13 50

" " Half calf, gilt or antique, . . 18 00

Augustus Neander, D.D.

Planting and Training of the Christian Church.
Edited by E. G. Robinson, D.D. (*in press*).

Commentaries, John, Philippians & James. 8vo., 1 75

History of Christian Dogmas (*in press*).

Adolphe Monod, D.D.

The Life and Mission of Woman. 12mo., . 50

Sermons—Monod, Krummacher, Tholuck, &c., . 1 00

W. W. Everts, D.D.

The Bible Manual. 12mo., ... 1 50

Childhood, its Promise, &c. 12mo., . . . 75

Manhood, its Duties, &c. 12mo., . . . 1 00

The Pastor's Hand-book. 18mo., . . . 50

The Sanctuary. 18mo., ... 42

Scripture Text Book and Treasury. 12mo., . 75

Rev. Chas. Buck.

Anecdotes—Religious and Entertaining. 8vo., . 1 50

Mrs. H. C. Conant.

History of the English Bible. 12mo., . . 1 25

Rev. C. H. Spurgeon.

Sermons, 1st Series. 12mo., ...	1 00
" 2d " 12mo., ...	1 00
" 3d " 12mo., ...	1 oc
" 4th " 12mo., ...	1 oc
" 5th " 12mo., ...	1 oc
" 6th " 12mo. . .	1 00
The Saint and Saviour. 12mo., . . .	1 00
Gems Selected from his Sermons. 12mo., . .	1 00
Life and Ministry. 12mo., ...	60
Smooth Stones from Ancient Brooks. 16mo., .	60
Communion of the Saints (*in press*).	

Francis Wayland, D.D.

Sermons to the Churches. 12mo., . . .	85
Principles and Practices of Baptists. 12mo., .	1 00
Domestic Slavery (Fuller & W.). 18mo., . .	5c

Richard Fuller, D.D.

Sermons. 1st Series. 12mo. (*in press*).

Mrs. Emily C. Judson.

Memoir of Sarah B. Judson. 18mo., . . .	60
An Olio, Poems. 12mo., ...	75

Geo. C. Baldwin, D.D.

Representative Women. 12mo., . . .	1 00

Mrs. S. R. Ford.

Grace Truman. 12mo., ...	1 00

Rev. Louis L. Noble.

Life and Works of Thomas Cole. 12mo., . . 1 25
The Lady Angeline and other Poems. 12mo., . 75

Rev. Sidney Dyer.

Songs and Ballads for the Household. 12mo., . 75

Mrs. Mary A. Denison.

Gracie Amber, a Novel. 12mo., . . . 1 25

Harriet E. Bishop.

Floral Home; or, First Years of Minnesota, . 1 00

Rev. Joseph Barnard.

Wisdom, &c., of the Ancient Philosophers, . . 75

Mrs. A. Lincoln Phelps.

Ida Norman. Illustrated. 12mo., . . . 1 25

David Millard.

Travels in Egypt, Arabia Petræa, &c. 12mo., . 1 00

John McIntosh.

The North American Indians. 8vo., . . . 1 50

Rev. William Arthur.

Origin and Derivation of Family Names, . . 1 25

Eliphalet Nott, D.D.

Lectures on Temperance. 12mo., . . . 1 00

Robert Turnbull, D.D.

Life Pictures from a Pastor's note book, . . 1 00

Rev. Matthew Mead.

The Almost Christian. 18mo., ... 45

John Frost, LL.D.

Wonders of History. 8vo., ... 2 00

T. J. Farnham.

California and Oregon. 8vo., ... 1 50

Life of Spencer H. Cone, D.D., . . . 1 25

The Life and Works of Lorenzo Dow, . . 1 50

Father Clark, the Pioneer Preacher, . . . 63

Homœopathic Practice, by M. Freleigh, M.D., . 1 50

The Napoleon Dynasty. Illustrated, 8vo., . . 2 50

Marble Worker's Manual, ... 1 00

Memoir of Thomas Spencer, ... 60

The N. Y. Pulpit, Revival of 1858, . . . 1 00

The Baptist Library. 8vo., sheep, . . . 3 50

The Living Epistle. Tyree, ... 60

Rollin's Ancient History. 8vo., . . . 1 50

The Words of Jesus and Faithful Promiser, . 37

Mrs. Thomas Geldart.

Daily Thoughts for a Child. 16mo., .	50
Truth is Everything. 16mo.,	50
Emilie the Peacemaker. 16mo.,	50
Sunday Morning Thoughts. 16mo., .	50
Sunday Evening Thoughts. 16mo., .	50

S. G. Goodrich (Peter Parley).

The Cottage Library. 10 vols., 18mo.,	3 75
Picture Play Books. 4to., .	75

Francis L. Hawks, D.D., LL.D.

Richard the Lion Hearted. 16mo., .	75
Oliver Cromwell. 16mo.,	75

Aunt Mary's Stories. 12 vols., .	3 00
The Little Commodore. 16mo.,	75
A Treasury of Pleasure Books. Gilt, .	1 50
Indestructible Pleasure Books, each,	20
The Illuminated Linen Primer, .	20
The Farmer Boy's Alphabet,	20
The Scripture Alphabet, .	20
Little Annie's Ladder to Learning.,	40

John F. Stoddard, A.M.

Juvenile Mental Arithmetic, ...	12
American Intellectual Arithmetic, . . .	20
Practical Arithmetic, ...	40
Philosophical Arithmetic, ...	60
Key to Intel. and Prac. Arithmetic, . . .	50

Stoddard & Henkle (Prof. W. D.)

Elementary Algebra, ...	75
University Algebra, ...	1 50

J. Russell Webb, A.M.

Normal Primer, ...	5
Primary Lessons, a Series of three Cards, .	1 00
The Word Method Primer, . . .	15
Normal Reader, No. 1, ...	12
Normal Reader, No. 2, ...	25
Normal Reader, No. 3, ...	38
Normal Reader, No. 4, ...	50
Normal Reader, No. 5, ...	75

Edward Hazen, A.M.

The Speller and Definer, ...	20
Symbolical Spelling Book. Complete, . .	20
" " " Part 1st, 288 Cuts, .	10
" " " Part 2d, 265 Cuts, .	1?

J. L. Dagg, D.D.

Elements of Moral Science. 12mo. . . . 1 00

Prof. Jean Gustave Keetels.

A New Method of Learning the French Language,   1 00
A Collegiate Course in the French Language,   .   1 00
Key to the New Method, ...   40
Key to the Collegiate Course (*in press*).

J. R. Loomis, D.D.

Elements of Anatomy, Physiology, and Hygiene, .   75
Elements of Geology, ...   75

Oliver B. Goldsmith.

Copy Books in Five Numbers, each, . . .   12
Gems of Penmanship, boards, ...   2 00
Double-Entry Book-keeping. 8vo., . . .   75

Exhibition Speaker, Fitzgerald, ...   75
Normal School Song Book, ...   38
History of the United States, Peabody, . .   75
Nelson's Copy Books, 5 numbers, each, . .   10
United States Speller, Miles, ...   12
Fitch's Mapping Plates, ...   30
Parley's Geography, ...   30
The University Drawing Book, ...   3 50

HOUSEHOLD LIBRARY.

Life and Martyrdom of Joan of Arc. By Michelet,	50
Life of Robert Burns. By Thomas Carlyle,	50
Life and Teachings of Socrates. By George Grote,	50
Life of Columbus. By Alphonse de Lamartine, .	50
Life of Frederick the Great. By Lord Macaulay,	50
Life of William Pitt. By Lord Macaulay, .	50
Life of Mahomet. By Gibbon,	50
Life of Luther. By Chev. Bunsen,	50
Life of Oliver Cromwell. By A. de Lamartine, .	50
Life of Torquato Tasso. By G. H. Wiffen,	50
Life of Peter the Great. Compiled by the Editor, 2 vols.,	1 00
Life of Milton. By Prof. Masson,	50
Life of Thomas A'Becket. By H. H. Milman, D.D.,	50
Life of Hannibal. By Dr. Arnold,	50
Life of Vittoria Colonna. By T. A. Trollope,	50
Life of Julius Cæsar. By Henry G. Liddell, D.D.,	50
Life of Mary Stuart. By A. de Lamartine (in press).	50

www.ingramcontent.com/pod-product-compliance
Lightning Source LLC
Chambersburg PA
CBHW060613030726
47498CB00005B/1659